A Heart Creek Second Chance

RETURN TO HEART CREEK - BOOK TWO

LYNN GALE

WINDSONG PUBLISHING CANADA

A Heart Creek Second Chance

A Return to Heart Creek Novel

This book is a work of fiction. Names, characters, places, and incidents are either products of the author's imagination or used fictitiously. Any resemblance to actual events, locales, or persons, living or dead, is entirely coincidental.

Published in April 2024 (e-book), Nov 2024 (print)

Digital ISBN: 978-1-7390527-9-9

Print ISBN: 978-1-0688010-9-9

Cover design by P.S. Cover Design & Author Services

Editing by Terri St. Clair

For my husband JP and my family
for your support and love.

For Katie O'Connor
for her encouragement and feedback.

For my island bestie Pat Maloney
I miss you!

Contents

Chapter One

Chelsea McCoy turned off the engine and sat motionless in her truck. Was this visit a good idea? Her heart thumped in her chest as she wrestled with her thoughts. The face in the rear-view mirror was pale, her green eyes pensive. She flipped her long red hair over her shoulder with a sigh, knowing she looked older than her thirty-two years. Who was this woman? At one time, Chelsea would have dashed off a flippant retort laced with humor. Now, she didn't know herself at all.

"And I prefer it that way," she insisted to the woman in the mirror. Much less painful than remembering the woman she used to be. Before Chance died. Before everything changed.

Time to get this over with.

Opening the truck door, she stepped onto the crisp hard-packed snow. A tall dark-haired man was walking across the parking lot toward her. Broad-shouldered and solid, he looked vaguely familiar but it took her a moment to register that it was Finn.

Her Finn.

Correction. Not hers. Not anymore. Not ever again.

Finn Buchanan stopped walking and raised his eyebrows. "Chelsea?"

"In the flesh. Dr. Buchanan, I presume? I didn't recognize you with your hair short and no beard." *Gosh, he looked good.* She'd forgotten how his six-foot, two-inch frame had made her feel safe, how his kind eyes had made her feel loved. She could almost feel his strong arms wrapped around her. *Whoa, girl.*

"What can I do for you?"

"I need to talk to you."

His hazel eyes narrowed. "About?"

"The county animal shelter."

"Ah, yes, the shelter. Bit of a dilemma there. Hey, how about we chat inside where it's warm?" He rubbed his bare hands together briskly. They sounded like sandpaper. "A bit nippy this morning."

Chelsea drew in a sharp breath. "Yes, that would be great."

Finn turned, walking toward the garage. "I live upstairs."

Chelsea hesitated – *was she doing the right thing?* – then followed the man she used to love into his home.

Be calm. Be calm. She mentally reviewed the list she'd painstakingly cobbled together for this meeting, welcoming the feeling of quiet resolve settling around her. She could do this. Her passion was animals. If not for herself, she could certainly do this for them. McCoys didn't give up. They might get close sometimes, but they always made it through. Except Chance. Pushing that painful thought away, she focused instead on her brother Mac. He'd found an amazing woman who was about to become his wife. Surely, Chelsea could find, well...closure for herself, maybe, hope for the shelter, and whatever else evolved. This first step was the hardest. *Keep it strictly professional, Chels. Forget your past with Finn, forget about Chance, and concentrate on what is important right now – the future of the animal shelter.*

Taking a deep breath, she tucked in her shirt and squared her shoulders. The apartment was small but neat and tidy. The tables beside the oversized deep brown leather recliner and sofa were piled with books and the electric fireplace had an autumn-hued woven rug in front of it. Chelsea relaxed slightly as she took in the warmth and coziness of the space. So very Finn. Or at least like the Finn she used to know. Before...

"Coffee or tea?" Finn derailed her train of thought.

"Coffee, please." Finn filled two large mugs from the pot, adding cream to hers without asking before handing it to her. Her heart pinged.

"You remembered."

"I remember everything." Finn's tone was wry as he lifted his mug. "Table or living room?" He paused for her answer.

"Table, please," Chelsea replied. At least having the table between them would hide her shaking legs and provide a safe barrier of sorts. She drank deeply, sighing when the rich coffee blend hit her taste buds and exploded into a myriad of sensations – the headiness of the sweet, rich cream weaving around the delicious bitterness of the coffee beans.

Finn raised an eyebrow as he too took a large gulp. Then he settled into his chair and gazed across the table at Chelsea. He didn't speak and the silence thickened until it became the awkward third person in the room.

Chelsea cleared her throat. "Finn." Her voice was hoarse. Raising a hand, she took another calming sip and a few deep breaths. *Stay focused, Chels. You've got this.* Her sweaty palms belied her thoughts as she wiped her hands on her pants and spoke again, her voice stronger.

"Finn, have you heard the news about the county animal shelter closing?"

Finn nodded. "Yes, I heard a few days ago."

"Okay, then you know they don't plan to reopen anywhere local. They are going to use the shelter in Montague instead."

"No, I didn't realize that. Huh. Montague is more than a hundred miles away. That doesn't make sense." He sounded as confused as she felt.

"I have an idea." *You can do this. You can do this.* "What would you say to opening a shelter here?"

Finn leaned back in his chair, clasping his hands behind his head. Classic Finn. He always liked to relax while thinking. He looked calm and even peaceful. No sign of what was going on in his mind. It was a trait that had always driven her crazy with impatience.

"Here? You mean here at the clinic? "He paused. "Haven't ironed out all the plans with Doc Olson yet," he added eventually, tapping his fingers on the tabletop.

Oh dear. She'd heard that Finn was taking over the practice and buying the clinic and land. Obviously, assumptions had been made. Embarrassment flooded her body.

"I thought it was a done deal. What are your plans then?" Her face flamed, realizing she was crossing a line by asking about private plans from a man she hadn't talked to in almost six years. "I'm so sorry, Finn. I assumed you were taking over everything from the Doc.... You know what they say about assuming. Sorry to waste your time." She rose abruptly.

"Chelsea."

She stopped but didn't turn around. Being around him was bringing up old hurts.

"Chelsea," he repeated. "You aren't wasting my time. Tell me more about what you are thinking. Sit. Please."

What to do, what to do? What could it hurt to let him know what she was thinking? She was here after all.

"If you're sure," she said, a little stiffly. She resettled in her chair and took a few calming breaths. In for a penny and all that. Her mind whirled as she tried to tame her thoughts into some semblance of order.

"That's an interesting idea, having a shelter here," he said when she hadn't spoken for several moments. "As of now, I don't know who will own which parts of the property. I'm not sure my financial situation will accommodate purchasing it all on my own. I had hoped to have a partner...." His voice trailed away.

A partner. Tears welled unbidden in Chelsea's dry throat. A partner for the practice. A partner for his life. Chance. And her.

"I can't do this. I have to go. I'm sorry to waste your time." She rose unsteadily, put her cup in the sink, and left the apartment. She could hear Finn saying something but all she could hear was a roaring and the word *partner* buzzing like an angry bee.

This was a bad idea. Stupid even. Silly girl.

Chelsea sat in her truck for a few minutes, letting herself recover before driving. Ridiculously, she half hoped Finn might follow her, but he didn't. *And why should he? You've made it perfectly clear over the last several years where he stands in your life. Absolutely nowhere.* She jammed the truck into reverse and hit the gas.

As she drove away, their conversation played in her mind. The warm spring sunshine that melted the last of the snow and gently dappled the trees did nothing to calm her frantic mind or aching heart.

She'd done the research and there wasn't a suitable and accessible area of land big enough for an animal shelter available within a comfortable driving distance of Heart Creek.

Except for the land around the vet clinic.

It was a double whammy – the forced relocation of the shelter due to the new highway and the county's budget cuts. As an animal health technician, she was familiar with Doc Olson's veterinary clinic. She'd done her practicums here and worked with Doc Olson on issues with Heart Creek Ranch's horses. Somehow, she'd managed to avoid Finn for the past several years but now with the old doctor retiring, those days were coming to an end, shelter issue or no shelter issue.

Finn Buchanan. Dr. Finn Buchanan, DVM. Doctor of Veterinary Medicine. The boy she'd loved when they were kids and the man she loved when they grew up. Until her brother Chance's death when everything changed. As his twin, she'd felt Chance's death deeply. It had taken months to recover a small semblance of normal, and even now there were dark days. She coped by keeping busy with the ranch, working for the shelter, and not thinking about the past. Now the past was apparently ready for her to deal with it – but was she ready to move forward?

Her family's ranch could have worked for the shelter relocation, but her brother Mac got there first with his idea of building a rehab center for rodeo cowboys. Part of her was annoyed and frustrated, but she knew the cowboy clinic he and Carrie planned to build at Heart Creek Ranch would be a welcome and beneficial addition to the ranch, the community, and Mac's life. She couldn't begrudge him that. The problem was what to do next. She had been so sure that Finn would buy everything Doc was selling. It never occurred to her that there might be an issue, financial or otherwise. She'd forgotten that Doc's previous partner had retired early and that Finn would be on his own once Doc left.

Like she was on her own. It wasn't supposed to be this way.

They were supposed to be together. Finn and Chance running the clinic. She and Finn married, with kids and animals and love. A family.

Everything was a mess. Again.

Still.

Finn muttered a few choice words under his breath. Chelsea had burrowed under his skin, again, after years apart. The beginning of a headache crept along the back of his head, winding around his temples. Rinsing their used coffee cups, he opened a cupboard searching for ibuprofen just as Chelsea spun out of the parking lot. He watched through the window, her frustration obvious by the way the tires dug into the snow and gravel. He smiled ruefully, shaking his head as he downed a couple of tablets. She always did have a flair for the dramatic. He missed her and her fiery temper and blazing emerald eyes.

Hang on! Where did that come from? He'd tried, quite successfully he'd thought, to put her into the part of his mind that seldom saw daylight. Now she was sneaking through the cracks. That couldn't be good. This wasn't going to end well for either of them.

Things hadn't ended well for them, his memory taunted, opening the door to a slew of places he'd rather not go. His headache escalated as he shrugged into his coat and headed to the clinic. He didn't have the time or energy to delve into the past. It hurt too much.

He'd heard the news about the county shelter on the radio while driving home from a call. As a large animal veterinarian, his days were long, he was often away from the clinic, but he loved the work. Now that Doc Olson was finally retiring, Finn's workload was increasing. The closing of the county shelter came as a shock. They'd all known about the new highway plans but thought it was a few years off. With the priority changes that the government made, the shelter had three months to find a new home or close. If it closed permanently, the rescues would be taken to Montague, a hundred miles away – almost two hours of driving – to the large shelter they had there.

Finn spent the next few days pondering what he could do to help. He didn't book appointments on Sundays – anyone with a problem was directed to an emergency practice half an hour away. Following a leisurely breakfast of eggs, bacon and toast, along with a few bracing cups of coffee, he tackled laundry and his personal version of housecleaning. Living in the apartment above one of the garages on Doc's property was a godsend. It had all he needed and was close to the clinic.

The idea of a shelter being built near the vet clinic stayed with him. It wasn't that he hadn't thought of it before, it was how to make it work. As he'd explained to Chelsea, he wasn't financially able to purchase the practice, house, and property on his own. Although Doc hadn't come out and said so, Finn knew that Doc was under the impression that Finn was going to take over the entire property. They had been advertising for a second veterinarian for months, but the pickings were slim. The combination of large and small animals wasn't necessarily what the prospects were looking for. Vets typically tended to focus on one or the other, not a combined practice. It didn't help that the partnership entailed a lot of driving and time spent away from the clinic. As a result, there was a delay and backlog of the small animal work. Thank goodness their veterinary assistant was staying on. She'd been there for almost five years and was invaluable to the practice. The receptionist was newer but already fit in well. What he needed was a full partner in the practice, and someone to run the clinic and manage the front end. And another vet assistant on top of that would be ideal.

Running his hands through his hair, he groaned out loud. Bottom line, what he needed was unlimited time and money. The reality was a little different, especially now with the animal shelter closing.

The county needed a shelter closer than the far end of the next county over.

Pouring himself another cup of coffee, he dug out his laptop. *First things first. Financials.* He logged into his bank account. He already had one plan in place, but he could redraw his five year business plan and see what made sense, now and in the future, including buying all the land available around the clinic. Then he could talk to Doc Olson and pump him for ideas.

As a relatively new veterinarian, Finn didn't have the means at his disposal to purchase everything, he needed a partner both financially and professionally. It was much too large a practice for one doctor alone. Truth be told, there was more than enough business for two or three doctors. Hopefully, a qualified vet would apply soon, and he'd have some helping hands. How Doc Olson had managed on his own since his partner retired more than two years ago was beyond Finn.

His thoughts swept to Chance and their plans for a partnership in a vet practice. And those thoughts led to Chelsea – their completely and utterly devastated relationship and ruined plans for their future together. All lost in an instant. So much anguish. So much pain. *Oh Chels.* Sorrow swept through him as if it were that day so many years ago. He'd tried so hard not to think about her, to forget the pain he'd caused her and her family.

The plans the three of them had made in university flashed across his mind. Chelsea, along with her twin and his best friend, Chance, and himself. They were going to finish vet school and then open their own practice including a large surgery, rescue and shelter, pet food business, as well as a small and large animal practice.

Chance's death killed that plan. And killed Finn's relationship with the only woman he'd ever loved.

Finn inhaled deeply, running a hand over his suddenly throbbing forehead. Chelsea. His one true love. Chels hated him and blamed him for her twin brother Chance's death.

Unfortunately, she wasn't completely wrong.

And now, here she was, right in the middle of the county shelter mess. He knew she wouldn't let the shelter idea go – one of her biggest strengths was her passion for what she believed in. *She used to believe in you.* Even while his headache continued to throb, his heart leapt. He still loved her and even though the odds were stacked against them, maybe this could be a bit of atonement for what had happened to Chance.

Doc Olson's clinic was perfectly situated on several hundred acres of land, with numerous outbuildings in good shape. Of course, county approval would be needed to convert those buildings into workable kennels and working areas but that was a mere blip on the dream's horizon.

It was worth a try. Wasn't it? For what was, and what could have been.

The next morning, Finn left the bank after meeting with the loans manager. With his current financial resources, he couldn't quite buy everything from Doc. He needed someone else to partner with. Vets willing to come out this far into the country and foot the bill for a partial buy-in were hard to come by. He needed a better idea, an alternate plan.

Chelsea had money. Or at least, her family did. The McCoy family owned Heart Creek Ranch which sprawled over several thousand acres. And she was qualified to run a rescue and shelter.

He stopped in his tracks in the middle of the street. Fortunately, Main Street wasn't busy at this time of day so being run over wasn't an issue. Continuing to his truck, he turned the idea over in his head, first this way, then that.

Chelsea was a certified animal health technician. She had planned on becoming a vet herself. She had access to money to help with the purchase – he knew the McCoy family would support her financially in that way. She was good with people and more importantly, good with animals.

She just wasn't good with him.

But maybe that didn't matter.

Once the idea crept into his mind, he couldn't get away from it. It kept popping up, taunting him, teasing him. Whispering hopeful thoughts to him. No matter what potential problem he came up with, a possible solution appeared.

He had to talk to Chelsea again.

Before that, though, he needed to organize his thoughts so that his proposal would be clear and concise. Simply a business arrangement. She could work part-time in-house at the clinic, handling the small animals and he could do the large animal practice and callouts. On the days the small animal clinic needed him for surgeries or what have you, she could take care of the shelter.

That evening, he sat down and wrote it all out. He built spreadsheets and different scheduling ideas, broke down what Chelsea's work requirements would be, and came up with a plan. He needed money but he also needed help. Chelsea could provide both. They just had to get beyond the agony of their past.

Easier said than done.

Chelsea was nothing like her fraternal twin. She was green-eyed and red-haired like their sister Avery, and fiery like their brother Mac, while Chance had been blond and blue-eyed like their dad, and even-tempered like their mom. Despite those striking differences, every time Finn looked at Chelsea, he saw Chance. His best friend. His university buddy. His non-blood brother. A good man cut down in his prime.

Could he and Chelsea do this?

They had to. Not only did the future of his veterinary practice depend on it but the area did too. The animal shelter that they could build together would mean a lot to the community.

First, he needed to talk to Doc Olson about the land and clinic deal. Hurdle number two and probably the simplest part of the whole venture.

Convincing hurdle number one – Chelsea – to work with him would be a whole different matter.

Chapter Two

Chelsea pulled into the parking area in front of the main ranch house. Gazing around, she was hit with a deep appreciation of the ranch's beauty and how much she loved this place where she'd grown up. The huge, sprawling ranch ran for as far as the eye could see and fed her need for space and breathing room. The fieldstone-fronted rustic ranch house, with its tiled roof, garnet red exterior, and wraparound cedar deck, emanated a warm, welcoming vibe, and felt like a hug every time she visited. She had intended to talk to her brother Ryker, but she realized she wasn't in the right headspace after her visit with Finn.

Changing her mind, she left the ranch and drove to her apartment in town. She needed to regroup her thoughts and figure out what to do next.

For the next few days, she went with her Plan A: searching again for any other local land on which to build the shelter. She scoured the area, sending out feelers to realtors and everyone she knew to get a lead on any land that was available to lease or buy. While there was certainly good land to be had, nothing was the size she wanted, or was located conveniently enough to work for a new shelter.

Nope, Doc Olson's land was the perfect fit. Not as spacious as Heart Creek Ranch, it still covered several hundred acres. There were already outbuildings in good shape that could be revamped. Access for the local community was ideal.

She had to talk to Finn again and see what could be worked out. The fate of the animals was more important than anything in her past. She had to look beyond that to the big picture.

When Finn messaged her right before suppertime the following day, she didn't know how to approach the shelter conversation again. His message was brief – simply "Can we meet for a bite?" For a wild moment, she thought he was asking her for a date, then she realized that would hardly be the case. She paused, conflicted. Part of her ached for him and what they'd had – more often than she would admit to, and usually when it was least expected. When her phone dinged again showing the words "business purposes", she relaxed and replied 'yes'. Then her mind started spinning. What kind of business purposes?

By the time she reached Homegrown Café, her anxiety was in full bloom. Finn was already there. He stood and waved when he caught sight of her hovering near the door. Her heart caught for a moment at the sight of his large frame and warm, smiling face. Swallowing quickly, she tightened her resolve and made her way through the crowded restaurant to his table.

"Hey, Finn." She slid into the booth opposite him.

He handed her a menu. "Thanks for meeting me on short notice." She gave him a slight smile, perusing the menu. She decided on soup and a biscuit, mostly to keep her hands busy. Her mouth was dry, and her tummy churned.

Once their orders were placed, Finn dove in to the reason he'd messaged her. "Chelsea, I have an idea. Could I ask that you hear me out before you jump in?"

At his words, Chelsea bristled. He was so, so *Finn*. Of course, she could wait until he was done. It wasn't like she had a habit of interrupting. Not often anyway. "My lips are sealed."

"I have a proposition for you," Finn continued. His eyes caught Chelsea's, his face turning beet red.

She wasn't sure whether to laugh or cry. Finn was just as nervous as she was! "For lil' ol' me?" she drawled.

Finn laughed a little and visibly relaxed. Chelsea's chest unclenched a bit, and she could breathe more easily.

"Let me try that again," Finn said wryly. "I've come up with a way to help the shelter and maybe help the clinic too. I want to offer you a share in the veterinary clinic, and a part-time job. I'm one hundred percent in favor of building an animal shelter near the vet clinic, to be managed by you."

Chelsea's mouth dropped open.

Finn continued to explain his plan. Partway through, Chelsea remembered to close her mouth.

When he finished, as she was about to speak, their server arrived with their food.

"Eat first," she managed to say. It would buy her some time to find words.

Inside, her brain whirled like a tornado. His offer stunned her. It was exactly what she wanted! The shelter would stay in Heart Creek! It was oh-so-tempting on many levels except for one big BUT – that he wanted her to buy into the vet clinic AND be a working partner in order to build the shelter. She would have to work side by side with Finn. That was a mountain of a BUT and one big hurdle.

On the pros side, financially she had savings she could use for the buy-in. She'd lived pretty frugally the last few years and her savings reflected that. She knew her brother Ryker would help her with the balance needed for the shelter. Money-wise, it could work. But the partnership idea and the working together? Ohhhh. That was a different kettle of fish.

Her mind ticked off the reasons against the idea. She'd spent years being angry at Finn. They had too much past to overlook. He was responsible for her brother's death. There was a murky grey mess of tangled emotions between them. She still loved him. *Whoa, what? Where did that last one come from?*

Was what he was offering even feasible? Could they make it work? Her head said yes, but her heart wasn't sure. She ached for Chance and his lost life. She ached for her family and their lost brother and son. But mostly, she ached for Finn and their lost love.

"Yes, okay."

Chelsea couldn't believe she had just spoken those words out loud and agreed to his plan. There were many reasons – or at least one big one – why she should walk away but somehow, she couldn't. Despite all the ways in which this plan could go wrong, if it went right – a very big IF – if it went right, it would be extraordinary.

An unfamiliar feeling that felt a little like hope warmed her heart.

"I'll talk to Mac and Ryker about the financial aspects," she continued, a smile forming of its own accord.

Finn's face beamed. "Fabulous. I brought you a copy of the financials, and my draft of how the partnership would look. We can talk more about it later. If you need anything else, let me know."

While they'd been speaking, he'd paid their bill. At the door, he smiled, and Chelsea's heart skipped a beat. *Finn. I have missed that smile.* Heady excitement raced through her body about the venture, and she wanted to hug somebody. Finn? She almost reached over to him before she remembered about Chance and hardened her heart. Finn handed her the paperwork he'd mentioned and left.

The next morning, it took a while to track Ryker down, but Chelsea was determined to talk to both of her brothers while she was still feeling positive about Finn's plan. Their plan, she amended. If this was going to work, it had to be together. Finn needed her help and her money. She needed his land and his outbuildings. They had to work as a team.

That last part was going to be tough.

Ryker was in the back quarter, talking to the ranch foreman, who rode away with a wave and a grin as Chelsea parked near the fenced area. She easily pulled apart the wire fence and scooted through, heading for her brother.

"What brings you out here today?" he asked as he enveloped her in a massive Ryker-sized hug.

Chelsea grinned as she disentangled herself. "You'll never believe it. Time for a coffee?"

"You read my mind," he admitted. "Meet you at the office." Mounting his horse, he took off for the big barn that housed the business office for the ranch. Chelsea climbed back through the fence to her vehicle and headed for the barn, her mind racing.

By the time she'd arrived, Ryker had two big mugs of steaming coffee ready. They settled into the conference room.

Chelsea took a long bracing sip of caffeine before beginning. "I've got an idea to run past you," she started.

"Okay, let's hear it." Ryker's face was open and interested.

Encouraged, Chelsea began. "I've been talking to Finn..."

Ryker's coffee sputtered out of his nose. Chelsea couldn't hold back her laughter as she handed him several napkins to wipe his face and the front of his shirt.

"Sorry," she said, in between guffaws. "Perhaps I should have started a little more slowly."

"You just caught me off guard," Ryker said. "Ow, my nose is burning!"

While Ryker moaned and whined, Chelsea took the time to rinse and refill his cup. By the time she was settled, Ryker appeared to have somewhat recovered.

"I'm okay," he said, in response to her query. "Please go on. I'm all ears."

Chelsea cleared her throat and started again. "Finn and I have been talking," she paused to make sure Ryker didn't inhale his coffee into his lungs again, and once assured he was fine, continued. "He has a proposition that I think you might be interested in supporting."

Ryker's eyes widened when she said *proposition,* but he nodded for her to keep talking.

She shared about her original visit to Finn to talk about the animal shelter idea, then their meeting last night and his subsequent offer for her to buy into the vet clinic and become a working partner. She detailed how they could then build the animal shelter near the clinic. She went over the initial financials he'd given her last night, noting that she had savings she could use for the buy-in. *Now the awkward part. The money ask from the family.*

She paused. Ryker remained silent, watching her.

"Would you and the ranch be willing to provide the balance of the funds we need to build the shelter, outfit it, and provide contingency funds should something not go to plan?" she managed to say. She gave him the amount Finn had felt would be enough.

"It's not an exact calculation," she hastily explained. "Mostly I just need you to say aye or nay so we can then get a full financial analysis done to ensure we have captured everything."

Ryker was silent for so long that Chelsea began to worry he would say no. Of course, Mac would also have to be included in this venture, but if Ryker was on board, she knew Mac would be an easy win.

He began slowly. "Chels, you'd have to work with Finn. Almost every day. In the same clinic."

Chelsea sighed deeply. "Yes," she acknowledged.

"And you would be okay with that?" Ryker looked at her, a questioning look in his eyes.

It was Chelsea's turn to pause. "For the sake of the animal shelter, yes."

"What about for your own sake, Chels?"

She met his gaze straight on. "I don't honestly, know, Ryker. But I am willing to give it a chance." Her eyes filled when she realized she'd mentioned her twin's name accidentally. She wiped her eyes and steadily gazed at Ryker. "It's time to move on," was all she could manage to say.

He patted her hand and grasped it in his big ones.

"We'll have to talk to Mac to get his buy-in," he said. "But based on what you've told me, and barring any surprises coming up with the analysis, I think it's a grand idea. Good for you, Chelsea. And Finn too. This is a win-win for the clinic and for the community. I'm proud of you."

Chelsea smiled, as her eyes filled again. This time, though, it was with relief and joy.

And hope. Actual hope, that unfamiliar long forgotten feeling, crept into her heart.

Finn's plan just might work.

Even with the financing potentially in place, and both Ryker and Mac onboard, Chelsea still wondered if she was making a big mistake. Trusting Finn, trusting herself around Finn, and making herself vulnerable was a big ask. Then she thought about the shelter and those animals they'd be helping, like Carrie's Winnie, an old deaf rescue dog who had captured everyone's heart. She was excited about working as a tech again and she knew that Chance wouldn't want her wasting her life.

It was time to take a giant step forward.

Even if it meant her heart could be broken again.

Finn was ecstatic when Chelsea called him with her news and promised to talk to Doc Olson as soon as he could. Later that evening, Finn called with his own news. Turned out Doc Olson was completely on board with selling the complete parcel and even offered to work reduced hours while they got the temporary shelter going, and the permanent one underway. A second vet was still needed as well as more help for the shelter, but they did have a bit of breathing room.

Chelsea met with the receptionist at the clinic and together with Finn, they went through the schedule, separating them into clients that Chelsea could deal with and those going to Finn and Doc Olson.

She and Finn met with the county office officials about the next steps for the new shelter development. They were given the forms and information needed to apply for the required permits. After the county meeting, they walked the property with Doc Olson, pointing out what could go where. Chelsea marveled at the extent of the land and the possibilities it offered. Stables and barns, plus an assortment of outbuildings, would provide all they needed for the temporary shelter. The future permanent shelter would be built on part of a vacant quarter section. There would also be an expansion for the clinic. It was mind-boggling and terrifying to know that even though financially they were covered, there was still a tight budget and careful pre-planning was necessary to ensure future solvency.

Chelsea's ideas kept coming. She read about a shelter on Vancouver Island that housed a rescue boutique where locals donated items to sell with the proceeds going to the shelter. She knew her sister Avery could design custom tags, as well as make natural shampoos for the animals to sell in the boutique. Finn loved the idea when she shared it.

On Doc Olson's property, soon to be their property, there was a second small building behind the clinic with office space and a furnished apartment. Finn offered it to Chelsea so that she could be on-site – part of their 24-hour service commitment to the community that Finn really wanted to maintain. Chelsea agreed and quickly made plans to move out of her apartment in town.

From her new living room, she could see Finn's place and the clinic. Convenient, cozy, and somehow comforting. Also terrifying to be so close to Finn.

Oh Chelsea. You still have it bad for that man. Despite everything. She might love him, but she wasn't letting him back into her heart. Ever.

The first few days working in the clinic were awkward, to say the least. Both Finn and Chelsea were in the office and couldn't avoid each other. It was unusually busy – word had gotten out of their plan and suddenly it seemed that everyone's pets needed a clinic visit. It had taken a few discussions but they managed to hammer out details and responsibilities to their mutual satisfaction. Doc Olson was happy to take care of the out-of-town calls initially so Finn could concentrate on the clinic while getting the new schedule up and running.

By the time evening came each day that first week, Chelsea was exhausted but happy. Working at the shelter had been great but being back in the clinic and fully using her animal vet tech skills was fabulous. And if she was truly being honest, she was starting to enjoy being around Finn. His amazing ability to be caring with both animals and owners touched her deeply. The ice around her heart began to thaw, day by day.

Avery was ecstatic about the rescue boutique idea – her sister was chomping at the bit about the potential and already had ideas. Chelsea giggled as she recalled the joy in Avery's voice. Everything was coming together.

Except for her and Finn, of course. That ship had sailed long ago.

Thoughts of Chance and what could have been came far less often than they used to, due mostly to the busyness of her days.

A few weeks after she moved into the apartment, she invited Mac and Carrie over to dinner to share their progress on Heart's Haven – the sanctuary for cowboys who needed a place to recuperate. They were hiring an equine therapist – a friend of Carrie's – as an added option for the cowboys – psychology mixed with horses. Not necessarily riding them but simply being with them. Horses were amazing animals and cowboys already knew that. It would be like mixing chocolate chips into cookie batter – just that little bit better.

She planned a simple supper of beef and chicken kebabs and salad, with her special bourbon pecan pie for dessert.

"Hello?" Carrie's voice rang from the front door. "Be right down," Chelsea answered. She ran lightly down the stairs. "We are going to eat in the covered area behind the clinic," she told Carrie. The apartment didn't have an elevator or a ramp – something Chelsea intended to remedy – so currently, getting Mac's wheelchair into the apartment was a no-go.

Hugging her brother tightly, Chelsea marveled at the changes in him the past few months had brought. His face was less gaunt, and his smile reached his eyes. He was recuperating from his rodeo accident quite nicely. Carrie had been so good for him.

She enveloped her future sister-in-law in a big hug, then knelt to pet Winnie, Carrie's deaf rescue dog. Winnie had been instrumental in alerting Mac and Ryker to Carrie's accident several months back. Without Winnie, Carrie might have died. "Hey, sweet girl," Chelsea cooed. They knew Winnie couldn't hear them, but they all spoke to her anyway.

The day was still warm and sunny so sitting outside would be comfortable. They were using the space hat Doc Olson had previously set up behind the clinic as a patio, complete with a propane barbecue and counter. Chelsea hadn't had any time to do anything to the area behind her apartment's building yet, but eventually she'd have her own little yard. Mac rolled himself to where he could look out over the back pastures, while Carrie helped Chelsea bring down the food and prep the table. Soon the tantalizing smell of grilled meat and vegetables filled the air.

"Where is the good doctor today?" Mac asked, lifting one eyebrow.

"I think Doc Olson is on a call in Ridgefield, "Chelsea answered, not looking at her brother.

Mac's sigh made her giggle.

"I mean the younger good doctor," he drawled.

Chelsea stiffened for a moment then realized it was a natural question now that she and Finn not only worked together but lived near each other.

"He's in town getting some supplies for the clinic," she replied smoothly. "He also planned on checking in at the animal shelter to see how things are going with the move happening soon."

"How is everything going with that?" Mac asked.

Chelsea spent the next few minutes bringing Mac and Carrie up to date on what they had achieved so far.

Mac whistled appreciably when she was done. "Great work in a short time," he said. "I'm impressed."

"The volunteers will have the temporary shelters in place within the next two weeks," Chelsea added. "The permanent facility will be built in stages, starting with the animal housing area and finishing with the offices. Okay, the food is ready, shall we dish up?"

The three ate in companionable silence.

At last, Mac sat back, rubbing his stomach. "Oh, that was good." He groaned.

Carrie laughed. "You certainly have your appetite back," she teased. In response, he threw his napkin at her.

Chelsea envied their ease with each other and the way they kept gazing over when they thought the other person wasn't looking. Ah, to be in love.

You were in love once, her heart reminded her. *Maybe you still are*, added a little voice deep inside.

Chelsea shook her head. Mac looked at her, his eyes narrowing.

"Just clearing my thoughts," Chelsea replied to his unspoken question.

"I'll dish up the pie and you can tell me all about Heart Creek Center for Cowboys. I'm so excited."

With that, both Mac and Carrie launched into the progress of the rehab facility they were creating for retired or hurt cowboys and rodeo riders. Chelsea loved how they took turns speaking, their thoughts definitely in sync.

"Can't wait to see it! When do you think you'll be ready for your first guests? Of the non-four-footed variety, I mean."

Mac chuckled. "We've hired a social media expert to help us get the word out. We've started a waiting list and so far, we've had inquiries but no takers. Once the building takes shape, and our website and brochures show our real vision, I think it will pick up. I have a few friends who I know would benefit."

Mac didn't sound worried about the future of the new rehab center. As a broken cowboy himself, he knew that the cowboys would be cautious and hesitant, at least at first. It was part of the therapy they needed – no pressure, no rushing. Just gentle love and caring while they healed and pondered what their next steps were.

"Hi there," Finn came around the corner by the house. "Smells amazing out here."

Chelsea hesitated for only a moment. "There are still warm kebabs," she offered.

"Yes, please join us," Carrie added, moving another chair to the table.

Finn's face broke out in a smile that wove through Chelsea's heart. "Yes, please! Thanks!"

He dished up a plate of food for himself and sank into the chair. Glancing around the table, he smiled.

"So how is everyone? Looking great, Mac, and Carrie, you are as beautiful as always."

Carrie blushed as she responded. "Thanks, you're looking pretty handsome yourself, big guy."

Finn laughed, looking down at his faded jeans and old work shirt. "Ah, you are into the casual type, I see."

Mac's voice broke in. "Hey there buddy, get your own girl. This one's mine!"

"I think I will do just that," Finn responded softly. Chelsea kept her eyes down, looking at the table, while she cut the pie. She could feel their gazes on her, and the back of her neck grew warm.

"Pie?" she asked, finally looking up.

"Yes!" all the voices answered together.

"I can't believe you inhaled that food already," she said to Finn.

"I'll have you know I'm a hard-working man, woman," Finn replied. "Yes, please, to pie."

His face was so open and sweet that Chelsea forgot herself. Gazing warmly into his eyes, she placed a hearty slice of pie on his plate.

"Hey, how come he gets the biggest one?" Mac retorted.

Chelsea's face flamed as an odd tension grew around the table. "Are you always this competitive?" she asked her brother pointedly.

"Heck, yeah!" both Carrie and Mac answered at the same time.

Everyone laughed and the jovial atmosphere was restored.

Chelsea, Chelsea, she grimaced to herself. *You have it bad for that man.*

Ba-a-a-d.

Chapter Three

For once, the county didn't take forever to approve the plans and issue the preliminary permits. The temporary structures arrived on a cold windy day. The rain and wind continued for a few days, pushing back the setup. Fortunately, they had built contingencies into their plan.

Finn marveled at how smoothly it was going despite the weather delay. Chelsea had shared her idea for the rescue boutique, and he agreed wholeheartedly, with the proviso that all profits benefitted only the rescue center. His chest tightened watching her face glow when she talked about it. The glimpses of the old Chelsea were bittersweet.

He couldn't believe how quickly his old feelings for Chelsea had returned. He felt like a smitten teen again every time he saw her face. He loved working with her in the clinic and admired her easy manner around both people and animals. If it hadn't been for that one night when Chance...*no point thinking about it now*, he admonished himself. *Can't change the past.*

Could he change what he thought would be his future though? Did he and Chelsea have a chance themselves? He wished he knew. Sometimes, he caught her staring at him, or smiling with that smile he loved so much, and deep in his gut, he knew she still loved him. But love wasn't what he needed. Forgiveness was the only thing that could change anything, and that didn't seem to be on Chelsea's agenda.

Not now, maybe not ever.

Still, a guy could hope. She crept into his dreams and his waking thoughts at the most inopportune moments. Maybe he could do something to move things forward. It's couldn't hurt to try, could it? He was already about as low as a man could get in her eyes. He had absolutely nothing to lose and everything to gain.

"Hey Chels," he asked, one day after an especially busy day at work. "Wanna grab a cold beer and some supper?"

Chelsea paused. *Yup, here comes the big no*, Finn thought.

"Love to," she replied. He almost choked at her words. *Glory be*!

"The café?

"Let's go to the new place – Mulberry Corner, right?"

"Yes, I've heard it was pretty good."

"Okay, give me a few minutes to shower and change, and I'll be good to go."

Finn smiled. "Go ahead. I'll lock up and meet you at the truck in forty-five minutes." He couldn't believe it had been that easy.

Chelsea stood under the hot water in the shower and groaned. What on earth was she thinking? Finn was a no-go zone. Danger, danger. Why had she agreed to go out with him? Because he mentioned beer and food, her tummy reminded her. Yup, two of her weaknesses, especially at the end of a busy workday. He knew her too well. She was just getting used to working with him. She hadn't considered socializing in her toolbox of 'how to deal with Finn feelings'. *Aargh.*

Forty-four minutes later, she locked her door and made her way down the stairs to the parking lot. Inside her nerves jangled and her breath caught when she saw Finn waiting at the truck.

Cowboy hat, face freshly shaved, faded jean jacket on top of a fitted black tee shirt and jeans – the man was drop-dead gorgeous. She wanted to step into his warm embrace and stay there, feeling his body heat and listening to his heartbeat. Forever.

She sighed. This was getting complicated. Way too complicated.

He smiled and came around to her side of the truck. "You clean up well," he said, eyes twinkling.

"So do you," she replied. He opened her door, and she stepped in. "Thanks."

"My pleasure, ma'am," he drawled, shutting the door gently.

As he strode around the truck to the driver's door, Chelsea drew a ragged breath. Running her suddenly clammy hands on her long jean skirt, she tried to stop the excitement building in her chest. *Remember Chance.* When a small voice inside asked *why*, she was shocked. *Why indeed? Because Chance dying was Finn's fault.* Then the soft question came back: *Was it though?* Totally confused, she paused her train of thought, just as Finn opened the driver's door.

Startled, she jumped, and Finn guffawed, his big laugh cascading through the truck.

"Sorry I scared you," he said softly.

Not you buddy, she thought. *I'm scaring myself.*

The restaurant was busy as they drove by, but Finn found a parking spot not too far away. Once again, he opened Chelsea's door, offering his hand as she stepped out. She shook her head, but when he held out his arm as they walked along the sidewalk, she accepted.

A small booth at the back had just been vacated. Gazing around, he nodded appreciably.

"Nice place."

"I love the old-timey feel to it and how warm the real wood feels."

Their server approached. "Welcome. Would you care for a beverage to start?"

"Beer, please, for both of us. Whatever is on tap is fine," Finn said, smiling at the young woman.

"You got it," she smiled back at him.

"Oh, and a glass of water, please," Chelsea added. "Tap water is fine."

"Make that two, please." Finn smiled again.

He glanced over at Chelsea. She had an odd look on her face.

"What's up?" he asked. "Did I miss a bit when I shaved?"

She looked thoughtful. "No," she said. "I'd forgotten how charming you can be."

Interesting, Finn thought. Interesting. He mugged and pulled a funny face. "Oh yes," he agreed. "Charming is my middle name."

Her grin made his heart jump. *Chelsea, I've missed you.*

They took their time with the menu, sipping their cold beers and chit-chatting about everything, but nothing in particular. Finn enjoyed watching Chelsea's face, her expressions changing as she discussed their latest four-legged visitors, and a few of the two-legged ones. He'd forgotten how wonderful it felt to be around her. He'd hidden it away when she broke up with him. Now, the feelings surged back, just as powerful as they always had been.

If only Chance's accident hadn't happened. If only Finn had been able to stop him. If only...

Chelsea's head cocked; her expression thoughtful as she gazed at him. He realized he'd drifted away with his thoughts. A flush rose on his cheeks as he brought his focus back to the beautiful woman at the table.

"Sorry, wool-gathering," he managed to say.

"About?"

Finn paused before he spoke. Was now the time?

"Chance."

It was out there. The name hung like a frosty cloud on the suddenly chilly air.

Chelsea's eyes filled with tears as she swallowed hard. *Not such a good idea then.*

"Finn..." she started to speak but Finn held up his hand to stop her.

"I'm sorry – not the time or the place," he apologized, suddenly desperate to salvage as much of this impromptu date as he could.

Chelsea bowed her head for a moment while Finn waited in awkward silence.

As she raised her head, the server approached the table.

"Are you ready to order?" she said pleasantly.

Chelsea nodded and they ordered nachos to share. Once the server left, they gazed at each other for a long moment. Finn could feel the pain in her heart right down to his toes. He reached across the table and took her cold slender hand in his. There were no words, he knew. Simply two souls who had lost someone dear to them, and in the resulting chaos, also lost each other.

Chelsea gently pulled her hand back.

"Avery is excited. She's already started trying different blends for shampoos," she said into the silence.

Finn accepted the change of topic for what it was, a small white flag. *Someday they were going to have to address the elephant in the room, but today was not the day. Would that day ever come?* Finn hoped so, otherwise there would never be hope for them which was not acceptable to him. Not one bit. Being around Chelsea added color to his life – color he needed as much as the air he breathed or the food he ate. There had been too much gray, too much dark, and too much emptiness, for far too long.

When their food arrived, they ate in comfortable silence, punctuated now and then with light conversation. Neither of them had room for dessert. The drive home was peaceful.

At Chelsea's stairs, he paused, about to say goodnight, when she leaned in and kissed him on the cheek.

"Thank you for a lovely evening," she said. She stepped forward and kissed him on the mouth before he could reply. Soft lips grazed his and for a slight moment she pressed in, a sweet promise wrapped in poignant memories of past kisses. Her hands grasped the back of his head. His breath quickened and his body reacted in muscle memory before she gently pulled away.

"Good night, Finn," she murmured, then walked up the stairs.

Holy farm cats on a tear. What the heck just happened? Finn waited until Chelsea closed her door and turned off her outside lights before he went into his own home, the feel of her lips still warm on his, and the feel of her hands lingering in his hair. *Wowzah.*

Maybe there was hope for them after all.

Chelsea leaned against the closed door, emotionally drained.

What was she thinking? Kissing Finn? Twice, no less! Good grief. She was so confused. It was easier when she'd hated him. When he was out of her life. *Was it though? Or was it cold and empty and lonely?*

She shuddered. It felt so good to kiss him. And right.

Oh my gosh. What was she going to do? She was falling for him despite her best intentions. And worse, she was betraying her brother Chance.

Exhausted, she craved sleep but once she got into bed, she lay there for a long time reliving the feel of Finn's lips, soft yet firm, drawing her in, making her want more. Memories flitted through her mind and her body. She missed him and what they had. Eventually, she slid into an uneasy slumber.

Amazingly, she woke up feeling rested several hours later. With two days off, she appreciated not waking up to an alarm. Glancing at her phone, she saw she'd missed several messages from her sister. She grinned. Avery hated waiting! Like most of the McCoy family, patience wasn't her sister's best trait. Even so, a long hot shower was appealing, and Chelsea took her time making her toast and coffee before settling in to give her sister a call.

"It's about time," Avery's tone bordered on annoyance.

"Slept in," Chelsea answered, between bites of her toast. "Whatcha got?"

The next half hour passed in a pleasant blur as Avery hit Chelsea with more ideas for the boutique. By the time they'd said their goodbyes, Chelsea's head was buzzing. She could already envision the shop, incorporating all things for pet lovers, with charming crafts on the walls, and stuffed animals tucked into hammocks around the room.

Thoughts of Finn tucked deeply away, she dressed for her day's adventures. First stop was the temporary shelter. Located a few hundred yards from the vet clinic, the barn they'd chosen to renovate was a great location. A temporary structure was being added on one end, providing more space for additional kennels. The barn originally housed an office used by previous farm managers – way before the vet clinic came to be – and there was a small but workable bathroom and large clean-up area already in place.

The warmth of the sun graced her face as she walked over, noticing the grass peeking through the barely remaining snow. Spring was well underway. She marveled at how quickly the contractors had made the barn into a usable space. Smiling at the two men working in the temporary area, she moved into the main barn area and gasped. The holes had been fixed and the area was clean and bright thanks to new lights running down the center of the barn and over what had once been stalls. The stalls had been renovated into kennels, small, medium, and large. Built-in cabinets were ready for supplies, and a large stainless-steel countertop shone in one area, flanked by animal washing bays, and more built-in cabinets.

The current county shelter had a capacity of three hundred animals. This temporary one would be able to house about two hundred fifty but the permanent one would be closer to five hundred. Her research had told her that shelters were usually built to accommodate about three percent of the human population of an area. With the county area population currently just under twelve thousand people, the ideal shelter capacity would be at least three hundred sixty. The population of Heart Creek had been in a holding pattern for the past few years, but she and Finn had determined they wanted to make sure that the permanent shelter would be able to handle any growth that might occur over the next twenty years.

Chelsea also wanted to make sure that no animal was ever turned away. Finn agreed. It was something they both felt strongly about, and she was grateful to have his support in that decision.

The area designated for the rescue boutique was part of the temporary structure she'd passed through on her way in. It was a large geodesic dome that would allow light in and provide a wonderful feeling of spaciousness to the little store. The permanent shelter would have a four-season area attached to the entranceway, offering the boutique, a check-out area for the animals who left for new homes, and a small office area for the admins.

It was already beautiful and Chelsea was thrilled that her idea had manifested into this space. Her idea and Finn's. Their shared vision.

Once again, tears blurred her eyes but this time, they didn't feel like acid burning her skin. They felt gentle, her pain being soothed by a sense of peace and gratitude. A new feeling for her, one she hesitantly welcomed, curious as to what had changed, what was changing.

Maybe she was learning to forgive Finn.

To forgive herself.

Was that even possible? Stranger things happened every day, all over the world.

She shrugged her shoulders and wiped her eyes. This was not the day to ponder the past. It was the time to embrace what was happening right now. And right now, she was going into town to load up on groceries and other supplies. She turned around abruptly.

Womppphh.

Her vision went dark and for a moment she thought she'd walked into a pole. Then she heard the muffled curse.

Nope. It was Finn.

"Oh my gosh, are you okay?" she cried. "I'm so sorry, Finn, I didn't know you were there." She stepped back and rubbed her face before peering at him through her fingers.

He was bent over, making odd noises. Oh no, had she hurt him?

He stood up, his face red and laughter mixed with strange noises gurgling out of his mouth.

"I'm okay, I'm okay," he managed to say, in between deep guffaws and moans.

Chelsea stood watching him, trying not to think about the warmth and breadth of this man that she'd run into.

"Finn, are you hurt?"

"Good morning to you too," he said. "I'm fine, really. You took me by surprise."

"Were you lurking behind me?" Her embarrassment came out as annoyance.

"God no," he said. "I was walking over here to see how things were going."

"Hmmmm."

"And I'm fine, really."

Chelsea still felt bad for walking into him head-on. "I'm planning to go to town shortly," she said. "Need anything?" She could have smacked herself for making the offer. She was trying to keep their personal and professional lives separate. *Professional only. No more kissy-kisses. Focus, girl!*

He smiled and his eyes sparkled. "Bananas?" he asked. "And maybe some of those little tomatoes if they have them? And chocolate, you know what I like."

Chelsea didn't know whether to laugh or cry. She did indeed know what he liked.

Darn it all anyway.

"Sure thing," she agreed. "See you later then. If you aren't home, I'll leave the bag on your porch." With that, she nodded her head and walked away.

The rest of the day passed at a comfortable pace. Chelsea picked up her and Finn's groceries, taking far too long to choose the nicest bananas and grape tomatoes. She stopped into Bellissimo Hair to see if Marina had time to trim her hair and agreed to head back in an hour for a cut. Getting herself an almond milk chai latte from Homegrown Café, she stuck her head into Pawsitively Purrfect to chat with Selina, the manager, about how the new shelter was taking shape. They had met earlier in the week so she could make sure that the new rescue boutique wasn't going to hurt Selina's sales in the pet store. Once Selina realized that the profits from the rescue boutique would be directly benefiting the shelter, she'd come on board with the idea. Chelsea planned to only carry donated items or items that the local pet store didn't sell.

Settling into the salon chair after having her hair washed and conditioned was amazingly decadent. Sipping the last of her chai, she relaxed, letting Marina's skilled hands clean up her curls.

Lost in her thoughts, it was a few minutes before she cottoned on that she was being talked about. Gazing in the mirror, Chelsea glanced around and took stock of the woman sitting across the room at another stylist's chair and talking on her phone while her highlights set.

"...those McCoys are into everything."

Chelsea's eyes caught Marina's, silently acknowledging they'd both heard the woman speak. Marina moved to say something, but Chelsea lightly shook her head. Marina nodded.

"Yeah, that new vet is a looker. I hear he grew up here? Figured Chelsea McCoy would be right in there. Always was the princess, that one, always getting every thing she wanted, not caring who it hurt. Remember her brother? No, not the crippled one, the other one. The one who died. I hear it was her fault...she never owned up to it though. See what I mean? Princess poor little ol' me...."

Chelsea's vision blurred, and she felt her stylist's hand on her shoulders.

"Never you mind," Marina said kindly, "That woman is a gossip and a backstabber. Don't take mind of anything she says."

Chelsea waved it off. "My fault, for eavesdropping," she managed to say. "You know what they say, eavesdroppers never hear good about themselves."

When Chelsea paid for her cut, she could tell the woman was watching her. Marina smiled as she gave Chelsea her receipt.

"See you next time, princess," Marina spoke loudly enough for the woman to hear.

Chelsea grinned, glancing over at the now red-faced woman still in her chair, before nodding at Marina. "Thanks, my friend," she said. "See you later."

She was still smiling when she got into her car, but her heart ached. The woman was being mean and gossipy, but she wasn't completely wrong. Not about the princess part or the McCoy bit. About Chance. Chance's death *was* partly her fault.

Hers and Finn's.

It was time. Time to get it all out in the open. Way past time. No more burying it.

No screaming, blaming, or crying.

Just talking calmly and rationally.

Time to have a conversation with Finn.

Chapter Four

Finn gazed out his kitchen window as Chelsea drove into the parking lot between their two places. A few minutes later, as she strode his way carrying grocery bags, he sensed that something had changed. Something in the way she walked and held her head high. He didn't know if the change was good or bad, but he had a feeling he was about to find out. Opening his apartment door in case she had planned to drop the bags and run, he saw her determined face and knew his intuition was right. Something had changed.

"Chels?" he asked.

"Do you have time right now? I'd like to talk."

"Sure, your place or mine?"

"Mine," she said. "Just give me a few minutes to put these groceries away and come on over."

She turned and left. The air felt heavy with emotion, and in his gut, he knew she wanted to talk about Chance and what had happened.

Time for the big-boy pants. They were going to have it out.

Ten minutes later, he stood at the bottom of her stairs, wondering if he'd given her enough time. When she opened her door and gazed questioningly down at him, he made his way up.

"Thanks for the chocolate," he said. "I brought some to share. Oh and here's what I owe you."

He placed money on her counter, but she didn't even reach for it. She handed him a mug filled with hot coffee and motioned him to the living room.

"So..." he smiled, hoping to lighten the mood.

It didn't work.

"We need to talk...about..." she paused.

His mind told him to give her space while his heart ached. He didn't want to go there either, but he knew they had to if they were to ever have a chance at love again. He waited calmly.

"We never really talked about this before," she continued slowly. "I mean, I guess we did but nothing was resolved."

"No," he agreed.

"We need to talk about Chance."

"Yes."

"You already guessed?" she wondered aloud.

"Yes."

She nodded and twisted her hands together. Then she looked up and caught him watching her. For a long moment, he tried to communicate with his eyes. She didn't change expression, so he wasn't sure it worked. Wasn't sure she could feel his love and compassion. He dropped his gaze.

"Chance died." Her voice was barely a choked whisper.

"Yes, he did."

"It was an accident..." It wasn't a statement yet not quite a question.

"It was an accident," he agreed.

"Was it though?" she asked slowly and distinctly.

Finn flinched at her tone despite trying to stay neutral, to stay calm.

"Yes, it was." His voice was firm and steady.

"Tell me about it."

"You know that I only know what you know."

"And why is that?" she asked, her eyes on his.

"Because I wasn't there."

"No, you weren't. And neither was I!"

"I know that, Chelsea."

"And why, Finn, why weren't we there?"

"Because we were making plans for our wedding."

"Exactly. We were making PLANS while my brother died."

Finn drew a deep breath. "Yes, we were. There is nothing wrong with that, Chelsea."

"Chance died because we weren't there to stop him. Or more to the point – YOU weren't there to stop him."

Finn's body trembled as the emotions of that night came flooding back, like a tsunami bearing down on him.

"Chelsea, your brother had a problem."

"Yes, he did! His best friend and his twin sister deserted him when he needed them most!"

Chelsea was crying now, wringing her hands and gasping.

"Chelsea. You know how stubborn he was. You know he would have driven that car that night no matter what."

"No, he wouldn't have. Not if we had been there." The words were so soft he almost didn't hear them.

"What?" Finn couldn't believe she thought that.

"He couldn't control his drinking, Chelsea. Us, or even just me, being there wouldn't have changed anything."

"We could have stopped him. You could have stopped him. Like you did before."

Finn's breath caught in his throat. *Like you did before.*

She knew. She knew that he had been the one to keep Chance in line when his drinking got the best of him.

"How long have you known?" Finn asked, his voice quiet.

"I only realized it recently," she admitted, in between hiccups. "But that doesn't change anything. It is OUR fault he died. Your fault for not stopping him. My fault for not realizing he had a problem back when it mattered. When I could have helped him."

Chelsea had accused him before tonight of being the reason Chance died. He hadn't had the heart to betray Chance's memories and set her straight on Chance's drinking habits. He'd let her believe what she chose to believe. She hadn't been in any state to listen.

"Chelsea, if it hadn't been that day, it would've happened another time. Chance was out of control. He'd been talking about quitting vet school. He was depressed."

"No, I don't believe you!" she screamed. "If you had been there, it would never have happened. If I had been there, I could have stopped him. We could have helped him."

Finn paused and drew a deep breath. His hands clenched as he remembered his own feelings of helplessness where Chance was concerned.

"Chels, he didn't want to stop drinking. He did not want to. I couldn't make him, and you wouldn't have been able to either. He couldn't stop it."

"He didn't want to die."

Finn didn't say anything.

"Finn, he didn't want to."

"Chelsea, I don't think he wanted to die. But I also don't think he wanted to live."

She stared at Finn, her mouth open, and her face unbelieving.

"You are lying." She insisted. "You just won't accept the blame."

Finn's heart cracked in his chest.

"Chelsea, if you think you are the only one who blamed me for not being there to save him, you are wrong. I blamed myself too! Yes, Chance died that night, and we weren't there to save him. But he would have died anyway! We were never going to be able to be there all the time to save him."

"You're wrong. You are wrong."

"Chelsea, that night a wonderful person died. Your beloved brother, your twin, my best friend. But you know what? He was broken. And now we're broken too. A big part of you died that night. And a big part of me. But I decided to live. To live fully and happily and completely. When are you going to stop blaming yourself – and blaming me – for being happy on the night he died? When we were making plans for our future. Before we knew he had died? Why are you continuing to punish us both? Isn't one death enough?"

Finn was silently crying, the tears thick in his throat and sliding down his face. He was tired. Tired of being blamed. Tired of blaming himself. Tired of being alone. So tired.

"Get out!" Chelsea said quietly.

Finn bowed his head, squeezing his eyes closed.

"Get. Out. Leave. Now." she repeated, a little more loudly.

Finn left and didn't look back.

Chelsea stayed in bed the next morning. She couldn't bring herself to get up, to face the day. Exhaustion racked her body after years of holding her feelings in and then releasing them. She felt no better than before the conversation with Finn; if anything, she felt worse. She was still conflicted about Chance's death. She'd realized in the past several months that Chance drank a lot back then. When she recalled different memories, she could see him there, nursing a drink, always with a bottle nearby. She knew he'd been depressed. She just hadn't seen how far gone he was, not in time to help him. Was Finn right? Was she using blame – blaming him, blaming them – as punishment for not being there to stop Chance's death? Was their relationship the scapegoat?

"At least he'd been alone in the car," she said out loud. "No one else died except the tree he hit when he missed the curve at high speed."

No one else died.

But that wasn't quite true, was it? She had died, deep inside and so had Finn. Their relationship had died. Their plans for their future together. Their love, their hopes, their dreams. Those had died when Chance died. How would Chance feel if he knew? Was that what he would have wanted for them?

If the situation were reversed, would she have wanted that for him? Would she?

She didn't know the answer. What used to be clear was muddy and distorted.

With those thoughts on her mind, she drifted into an uneasy sleep once more.

Finn spent the next day watching Chelsea's apartment for signs of life. He knew she needed time to process, but he wanted to keep watch in case she needed him. In the meantime, he cleaned his apartment and caught up on laundry before settling down to read a book, one eye on the words, one eye on Chelsea's door.

When he saw the kitchen light go on later that evening, he breathed a sigh of relief. He had no idea what was going to happen next after yesterday's conversation, but at least she was okay. That was a good first step.

He wasn't clear on his feelings. Old fragments of guilt merged with missing his best friend, losing the love of his life, and holding himself responsible for Chance's death. For letting Chelsea pull away from him. For allowing them both to deal with the aftermath alone. In the years it had taken him to realize that what he'd said to Chelsea was indeed true – that even if he had managed to save Chance that fateful night, he might not have been able to another time. He wished he'd known to connect Chance with mental health therapists or addiction counselors, or even AA but he wasn't sure how open Chance would have been to any of those. Chance had his own path to follow. Even with his troubles, he was still responsible for himself.

Finn's emotions were raw and vulnerable, his body ached and his thoughts circled in an endless spiral. He and Chelsea were reliving Chance's death repeatedly. He'd tried to make his own humble and tentative peace with it. Could she? And if she could, would she take a risk on him? On what they'd had? On what he knew they still had?

He didn't know the answer to any of those questions.

He wondered if this would affect their professional relationship and business contract. It was the biggest fear he had – that everything would be irrevocably broken. It was more than he wanted to think about right now. All it did was make him feel worse.

He'd see how Chelsea was in the morning when they were back at the clinic. With the new schedule, it would only be one day working together then he was covering the fieldwork for a few weeks. A break from each other might be a good thing.

As it turned out, the next day started with a bang. First, they had a dog hit by a car, then two euthanasia cases in a row – old sick cats who had survived surgeries but were fading quickly. It was after lunch before he ran into Chelsea and even then, it was only in passing as she paused at the desk to see who was next in the waiting room.

Finn met with Doc Olson before the old doctor took a few days off then headed into town for errands. When he got back, the clinic was closed for the day. He gazed up at Chelsea's drawn curtains and dejectedly headed home. *Give her time. Be patient.*

His first callout came a few minutes later and shortly after, he was heading north to the Olineski farm.

Chapter Five

Chelsea heard the truck pull away from the clinic and realized Finn had gone without saying goodbye. That stung a little. A lot, she admitted to herself. It had been a busy day in the clinic and none of them had taken a break. Tossing together a chicken veggie salad and a big cup of tea, she tried to settle in with a blanket and a book.

She picked at half her salad before succumbing to the fact that she wasn't hungry. Her eyes kept dancing off the pages of her book, and she couldn't seem to relax. Her cell phone vibrated, announcing a call. She glanced at the caller ID. It was her mom.

"Mom?" Chelsea said.

"Hello sweetie," Elizabeth McCoy's voice brought moisture to Chelsea's eyes. She missed her even though Elizabeth had visited at Christmas, not that many months ago. She'd spent the past few years living in Lethbridge, caring for her older sister Agathe.

"Some sad news, I'm afraid," Elizabeth continued. "Aunt Agathe has passed away."

Oh, her poor aunt. She had suffered many years with dementia and the past months had brought a litany of physical issues as well.

"I'm so sorry, Mom."

"Me too," Elizabeth went on. "I will miss her. Very much. Now tell me how you've been, my dear girl."

To her utter horror, Chelsea burst into tears.

"Chelsea?" her mom's voice cut through her anguish. "Are you okay, love?"

"Oh Mom," Chelsea wept. "I'm...so confused."

There was a pause on the phone.

"Is it the shelter? Ryker told me about your plan with Finn," Elizabeth said. "I think it's marvelous and I support you whole-heartedly."

"Thanks," Chelsea blubbered. "No, no, that part is fine."

"Are you not well?" Elizabeth asked next.

"I've been thinking a lot about Chance," Chelsea managed to squeeze out the words.

"Ah," Elizabeth said. "Our sweet Chance."

"Mom, can I ask you a question?"

"Of course."

"Did you blame Finn for Chance's death? Or me?"

"What? Why, of course not, Chelsea. Why ever would you think that?"

Chelsea paused to wipe her nose before answering.

"We weren't there to stop him. To save him."

Elizabeth's voice was firm. "Chelsea, my love, no one was going to be able to stop our Chance. That boy was strong-willed and stubborn. His drinking was out of control. He knew it, I knew it, and Finn knew it. We tried to help him but he didn't want to listen. He refused to accept that he had a problem."

"I didn't know it until recently," Chelsea admitted in a small voice.

"You always thought Chance was perfect, lovely," Elizabeth reminded her, her tone gentle.

"Hmm. I guess I did," Chelsea agreed.

"He wasn't. No one is. And no one, not even me, was going to be able to stop him until he decided to do so himself. He didn't want to go to AA, he didn't want to stop drinking. He kept telling us that it was under control and we were overreacting."

"Okay," Chelsea said, her voice small.

"Chelsea, have you been blaming yourself all this time? And blaming Finn? Is that why you broke off your engagement?"

Chelsea swallowed hard.

"Yes, I think so."

Her mom's sigh flowed through the phone. "Honey, I wish I'd realized that sooner. Believe me when I say that there was nothing you – or Finn – or I – could have done. We all have our demons, Chelsea. Alcoholism is a terrible disease. I think, eventually, Chance would have come to terms with accepting help to fight it but at the time, it was stronger than he was. His death was a horrible, terrible accident."

"Really and truly?"

"Really and truly. Cross my heart."

"Oh Mom, I've wasted so much time."

"Well, then, do something about it, dear," Elizabeth said frankly. "In the meantime, my love, I have a service to plan. Aunt Agathe left specific wishes that I intend to adhere to. I'll be in touch with more details."

"Mom – do you need help?"

Chelsea could hear Elizabeth's smile over the phone. "No, dear, but thank you. We've known this was coming for several weeks. I am fine and your cousin Braden is here to help as well. You take care of you. I love you!"

"Thanks, Mom! I love you too." Chelsea's voice was lighter.

"Oh, and Chelsea? Say hello to Finn for me. I've missed that young man."

Me too, thought Chelsea. *Me too.*

"Yes, I will," Chelsea promised and ended the call.

For the next week, Finn got home well after dark and left each morning before dawn, as he attended to calls. While he enjoyed seeing the people in the area, he was surprised to discover he missed the steady pace of the clinic and being home for supper every night. Of course, that had everything to do with Chelsea.

Driving around the county allowed him lots of time to think. He still loved Chelsea, that was a given. He would do anything for her, including removing himself from her life to make her happy. Even if it broke his heart. Again. He'd lost her once. He could handle losing her again if that's what it took.

After several false starts, he mapped out an option they both could work with. Even though he preferred the in-town clinic work, he would stick with doing the fieldwork and change the search for a vet to include only the in-town portion of the practice. Doc would be fine to help for another month or so, and it might make the position more appealing to applicants if they knew it was ninety-nine percent in-town.

With him away most of the time, Chelsea could continue working part-time at the clinic as well as run the shelter, without fear of running into him. He'd make sure any in-town time was opposite her work schedule so the likelihood of working with each other was lessened. Their business arrangement could stay what it was. That would give her time before the shelter moved permanently and she took over its management to come to terms with their re-broken relationship.

It wasn't a perfect plan, but it came close. He could live with it. His heart was telling him no, don't do this, but his mind was set.

Once everything was in place, he'd present the plan to Chelsea. If she knew he wouldn't be around the clinic, it would ease any worry she had about running into him. Both of them could continue in their roles with the clinic and the shelter. Nothing had to change professionally.

Of course, on a personal level, they were broken and this time, probably irreparably.

Chelsea couldn't wait until Finn was home for more than a night. Since the phone call with her mother, the weight of Chance's death had lifted, and she couldn't believe how light she felt. Finn was right – she had allowed part of herself to die. He was right about many things.

Oh Finn. She'd been so wrong, and she hoped he would forgive her. It took everything she had not to phone him. She knew her revelation was better delivered in person, face-to-face. At least then he couldn't hang up on her.

When he pulled into the clinic parking lot a few days later just before lunchtime, she was beside herself with joy. She dashed outside to meet him by the truck.

"Welcome home," she said, when he stepped out of the vehicle.

He reached into the back for his duffle. "This is a surprise," he said easily.

Chelsea shrugged. "I was hoping we could talk."

"I'd love to but first I desperately need a shower. I have an interview. I spoke with a young vet from Calgary who is interested in joining us. I'm meeting him in town this afternoon."

Chelsea's face fell but she recovered.

"Oh, that's great," she responded. "Maybe later or tomorrow then?"

"Sounds good," Finn replied and walked towards his apartment.

Chelsea's good mood morphed into a funk as she walked back to the clinic.

"How's the boss?" Gloria, the vet assistant, asked.

"Good, good. I guess he's interviewing a possible new doctor this afternoon."

"Oh, that's right," Gloria answered. "Craig Willmont. He'd been interested in the job before but wasn't too keen on the field work side. Now that Finn has changed the position to be in-town only, Craig's back on board."

Chelsea frowned. "What do you mean changed the position?"

Gloria's smile shrunk a little. "You know – with Finn deciding to stay in the field permanently and not switch off with another vet."

Wait, what? That was news to Chelsea. Big news, in fact.

"You'd think he'd have told his business partner," she mumbled.

Gloria looked embarrassed and glanced over at their receptionist.

"I'm sorry, Chelsea. I had no idea you didn't know."

"Not your fault at all," Chelsea hastened to assure Gloria. "I probably did know but it slipped my mind. Let's go check on that sweet mamma cat in the back. How is she feeling?"

By five o'clock, Chelsea was fuming. How could Finn not tell her what he was planning? Him staying out in the field was a big deal. What would that do to any possible relationship they might have, if he was gone all the time?

Wait and talk to him. He'll have a reasonable explanation for this. He probably just hadn't had time to tell her in the excitement of finding someone interested in the job. Even though he'd had time to tell their vet assistant and receptionist. Arrrgh.

The next morning when she rose, Finn's field truck was gone. She sighed. *Rats and double rats.*

The clinic was abuzz when she walked in. The receptionist beamed at her.

"Good morning, Chelsea. Isn't that great news about Craig?"

"Oh yes, "she agreed woodenly.

"And he can start almost right away. I'm looking forward to working with him. He's got great credentials and from what Finn says, sounds like a good fit for us. He called Gloria and me last night to let us know."

"Great fit for us," Chelsea agreed. "Great, great."

She headed to the back to prepare for the day, her mind in a fog.

"Isn't that great news about Craig?" Gloria, the vet assistant, exclaimed, as Chelsea gave the gleaming back counter an unnecessary swipe with a cloth.

"Oh yes. Great, great."

Gloria looked at her oddly. "Are you okay, Chelsea?"

"Yes, yes," Chelsea said. "I'm just freaking great."

At the end of the day, exhausted from smiling, she locked the clinic doors. Finn's truck pulled up as she made her way to her apartment, but she didn't bother to stop. She thought she heard him call her name but ignored it.

He can wait.

She stood in the hot shower for a long time, thinking. Why didn't Finn tell her his plans? She heard knocking on her front door but didn't acknowledge it. She wasn't up to facing him or anyone else.

She was in her jammies, curled up on the couch when she heard knocking again.

Sighing, she realized he wasn't going to give up.

She opened the door, just as he was heading down the stairs. "Finn."

He turned and headed back up.

"Sorry to disturb you," he said. "You wanted to talk? Sorry. I've been a bit preoccupied."

Anger, disappointment, and frustration warred with the need to share her epiphany about them, about him.

Gazing at his handsome face, Chelsea threw caution to the wind.

"Come in, please," she invited, smiling.

"Okay," he agreed but his face was uncertain.

"Drink?" she offered brightly.

"No, thank you."

She girded her loins and gathered her thoughts. "Finn, I've been thinking a lot..."

"Me too, Chels."

"Yes, well, I want you to know that I don't blame you anymore for Chance's death."

Finn's eyebrows went up, almost to his hairline. "Oh, that's nice," he replied, slowly, his voice quieter than usual.

Chelsea frowned. "Nice? Nice? I forgive you, Finn. That's not *nice*, it's *fabulous*!"

"Oh, sorry. Thank you for forgiving me. I appreciate that."

What was happening here? This wasn't going the way Chelsea had planned. She tried again.

"Finn, you were right. It wasn't your fault or my fault – it wasn't anybody's fault, It just was what it was. I forgive you. It's a huge thing."

Finn's mouth pursed and his eyebrows furrowed. "You forgive me for Chance's death?"

There, now he was getting it. However, from the look on his face, Chelsea didn't know what was going on in his mind.

"Yes, and I am incredibly sorry I wasted all these years being angry."

"Me too," Finn said slowly, biting out each word as if it physically hurt him to speak.

"Chelsea, I've decided that I am going to stay on fieldwork permanently. Today I hired a vet who will look after the in-town work. That way you and I can continue our business arrangement but not have to see each other."

"Yes, yes, I heard, "Chelsea impatiently said. "Craig Willmont. Starting in a few weeks."

"Oh the girls must have told you."

"Well, it sure didn't look like you were going to," Chelsea retorted, still hurt by the omission.

Finn looked askance at her. "Chelsea, I am completely confused. You told me to get out. I thought you didn't want to be anywhere near me. This plan will solve that."

Chelsea wanted to stamp her feet like a three-year-old. *Why was this infuriating man not understanding what she was saying to him? This had gone so off the rails!*

"Finn. I. Forgive. You." She repeated slowly. "I forgive you. Didn't you hear me say that just now. We don't need a plan."

"I get that but it doesn't change anything," Finn replied. "There is too much that we can't get past."

"Yes, we can! We have gotten past it. We can be us again. I realized I was wrong for blaming you for Chance dying. It wasn't your fault. Don't you still love me?" Chelsea demanded.

Finn paused for a long time, not saying anything.

Chelsea's fear and anguish threatened to choke her. Her heart pounded. *What was going on.? Oh god no. Unless the worst thing possible was happening. Maybe he didn't hear what she'd said.* "Finn...do you still love me?"

He shook his head. "No, Chelsea, I don't. I'm sorry."

Chelsea couldn't believe her ears. He didn't love her anymore. Her vision blurred and she gasped out loud.

Finn stood abruptly. "Bye Chelsea."

She didn't even try to stop him. She just sat there, numb and shaking.

She was too late. Too late. Too late for love.

Chapter Six

It took Finn three tries to close Chelsea's door. He stood outside, shaking. He wasn't quite clear on what had just happened. He replayed their conversation in his mind, unreasonable anger and frustration warring with his confusion and causing his head to pound. Bit and pieces of her words drifted in and out of his mind. *So, she finally forgave him, well whoop-dee-doo. Wasn't he supposed to be the one to forgive her for blaming him in the first place? Where did she come off forgiving him?*

He just out and out lied to the love of his life. Was he nuts? She said she loved him but somehow those words weren't penetrating. His head hurt and his heart thumped. Maybe he was having a heart attack? His left arm felt fine, so no. But something was going on with his heart and it wasn't good. He kicked the railing with his toe and trudged down the steps. He'd said what he'd come to say and it didn't matter. *Aargh.* Creating space between them would be the best solution. He'd already offered his apartment to Craig and found himself a place in town to rent, at least for the interim. It would be easy enough to head to the clinic from town to stock the truck with the veterinary supplies as he needed them. As for him and Chelsea – well, that was done. Over. Finished. Now he had to pack and get away from here, the sooner the better.

Chelsea was in shock. Finn didn't love her anymore. What a fool she'd been. She should have kept her mouth shut and her heart sealed. She loved the clinic, with or without Finn. She wanted to run the shelter. Nothing had changed, except any possibility of reconciliation. That was a done deal.

Finn was off his rocker. Wasn't an apology what he wanted? Wasn't that enough to make him love her again? And what about her declaration of love? He'd acted as if he hadn't even heard her. Was was that all about?

"Focus on work, Chelsea. You don't need Finn."

She could do this. She would do this. With or without Finn's love.

Diving into her work over the next few days, she spent time catching up on the temporary shelter's progress and paying a visit to the county shelter. She walked through the aisles saying hello to the rescues, pausing for pets and hugs where she could. Her heart ached for these sweet souls. She longed for a pet of her own and promised herself she would get a dog sooner than later. She was looking for comfort, but their loneliness echoed her own.

She was in the back of the clinic checking on the overnighters when the door chime indicated a client. Knowing the receptionist was out for a few minutes she headed to the front door only to stop dead in her tracks.

"Hello," the tall, blond and gorgeous man standing there said cheerfully. "I'm Craig, the new partner. And you are?"

"Chelsea, I'm Chelsea, Finn's other business partner," she managed to say, her heart hammering in her throat. Holy heck. Craig looked just like Chance. *Oh no, oh no.*

Numbly, she showed him into Finn's office and left him to get settled. Watching him covertly from the receptionist's desk, she dimly realized the resemblance was superficial, but it was there in the blue eyes, the big toothy grin, and the mop of golden hair.

"He's kinda handsome," Sammy, the receptionist, whispered into her ear, nearly causing Chelsea to jump out of her skin.

"Don't sneak up on me like that!" Chelsea hissed. "You nearly gave me a heart attack."

Sammy grinned. "Sorry, Chels," she giggled. "I'm back at my desk. He sure brightens up the office."

A moving van carrying Craig's personal effects arrived that afternoon. Chelsea knew from the office girls that Finn had moved out of the apartment but kept her distance. Her heart was already broken. Again. Why add fuel to that fire? Or kick a dog when he's down. Or, well, really any other cliché that came to mind. Move on or move out. Then she got angry at Finn all over again.

With that in mind, she approached Craig when the moving van pulled away. "Can I interest you in a welcome to the practice supper?" she offered. "There're a few great eateries in town."

Craig agreed to meet her in front of the clinic after work to head to town. Chelsea took her time to change into dressier clothes. She needed to feel better about herself, and sometimes nice clothes helped. *And sometimes they didn't.*

As they pulled away from the clinic, Finn's truck pulled in. Drawing up beside her, he indicated for her to roll down her window. She sweetly smiled as she did what he asked.

"Hello there," Finn leaned over to gaze into her vehicle. He looked past her to the passenger seat and nodded at Craig then turned back to her. "I see you've met Craig." His eyes narrowed as his gaze met Chelsea's. She didn't back down – she forced herself to continue smiling at Finn.

"Sure did. We're heading to town for supper."

"Ahh," Finn replied. "Maybe I'll join you...."

Chelsea inwardly panicked and made a quick decision. "Oh, I'm sure you're tired," she replied smoothly. "Next time." She floored the gas and pulled away from Finn's truck. She watched him in the rearview mirror as they drove away.

Craig chuckled and said "Oh, that's the way it is, eh?"

Chelsea snuck a glance at him. "What's what way?" she said, innocently.

"How long have you guys been together?" Craig asked, instead of answering her question.

Chelsea's mouth dropped open.

"Oh no no no, "she retorted firmly, with a laugh that even to her ears sounded forced. "We are so not together. You've got it all wrong."

Craig looked at her and tilted his head. "Do I, though?" he said softly.

Chelsea swallowed emotions better left unsaid and nodded.

***

Finn glared at the departing truck. So that's how it was going to be, he fumed. The first time his back was turned, Chelsea turned to the new guy. He parked his truck, seething.

Ummm, you told her you didn't love her. What did you expect?

"Not for her to pick up with the first Tom, Dick, or Craig that showed up," he grumbled aloud. "What's that all about?"

She should just sit home and be alone then?

"Yes, darn it," Finn snapped. "No, heck – geez, I don't know."

You are jealous. "I am not jealous!" *Yes, you are. You still love her.*

Finn rested his head on the steering wheel. Dang it. *He still loved her. Keeping his distance was not going to protect his heart. Dang it.*

He banged his hand on the horn repeatedly, swearing. The horn stuck and wouldn't turn off. Drat and drat again. He jumped out of the truck after opening the hood lever, trying to quiet the horn. Finally successful, he closed the hood. Walking back to the driver's side of the truck, he paused to gaze at his reflection in the side mirror.

What on earth had he been thinking? His solution seemed perfect in theory. Now all he would think about was Craig and Chelsea together. How had it gotten so messed up?

Craig was delightful company at dinner, but it took everything Chelsea had to smile and maintain her side of the conversation. Once coffee had been served and dessert declined, she glanced at her watch.

"Somewhere else you have to be?" Craig asked, noticing her glance.

"I do have some shelter paperwork to do."

Craig nodded and asked for the bill. "Oh no," Chelsea shook her head. "I invited you, it's on me."

"Thank you," Craig replied. "It's not often I am treated to a meal." Chelsea was glad he didn't argue with her. Finn certainly would have. *Oh Finn. I miss you so much. You idiot.*

The ride back to the clinic was quiet but not in an awkward way. Craig headed for his apartment and Chelsea to hers.

She fell asleep on the couch not long after.

Chapter Seven

Chelsea's phone buzzed but she let it go to voicemail and pressed her head more deeply into the pillow. A sharp knock on the door startled her and she stumbled off the couch to open it. After a restless night filled with dreams of Finn and an impossible happily ever after, she was barely functional.

"Finn?" It was still dark! Why was he beating down her door in the middle of the night?

"There's a fire at the old shelter. Some of the animals have escaped. They're going to bring the others here to the clinic. Get dressed. We need to help."

Wide awake, Chelsea threw on warm clothes and hastily laced her hiking boots before slipping into her coat. As an afterthought, she grabbed packaged snacks and snagged two bottles of water.

Finn pulled out the second she climbed into the truck.

"Not sure how the fire started but I guess it's bad. We called as many volunteers as we could to move the animals. The fire department is on the scene managing the blaze, but the animals are an issue. Peace officers are helping, but they need more help."

They could see the blaze well before they pulled up to the barricades set up around the perimeter, the orange glow brilliant against the dark sky.

"Evening, Chief," Finn addressed the soot-streaked fire chief.

"Finn. Fire's not under control yet so can't let you any closer. Most of the animals that escaped headed that way. We aren't sure how many." Pointing towards the foothills, the chief shook his head. "Not sure how they'll fare but at least they are momentarily safe from the fire."

"Thanks. Chelsea and I will head that way. Craig and the girls are coming to take some animals to our new place. I have my radio for updates."

Reaching into the back of the truck, Finn grabbed a couple of portable cages, several leashes, and two backpacks. Chelsea donned one pack and Finn the other before heading into the darkness.

"There are headlamps in my bag," Finn directed. She rummaged and found them each one, pausing to attach them before they set off.

A few hundred yards up the way, they spotted a small glow in the underbrush. Finn motioned Chelsea to stop, and he crept towards the site after lowering the brightness on his headlamp. A few moments later, he emerged with a large tabby cat in his arms.

Quickly setting up one of the cages, Chelsea wrangled the terrified feline into the cage, then slid the straps over her shoulder.

Continuing their trek, they walked in silence, wanting to hear any noises that would alert them to more animals. They followed shrill yaps into a hilled area where they found a small dog tangled in the bushes. The dog was frantic as they approached but Finn was able to free the dog and clip on a leash. The dog scratched at Finn's leg until Finn picked it up, receiving licks and small growls in return.

Finn radioed their finds and advised that they would continue their search a while longer before returning to base camp with their animals.

Chelsea gazed around in awe. The night was gorgeous, the dark sky lit with shimmering stars and no moon. The moon would have aided their search but may also have led predators to their unfound escapees.

After more than an hour, Finn stopped. "Let's take a short break and reassess."

Chelsea was relieved to set down her backpack and small kennel. The load wasn't heavy, but it was cumbersome. Digging into his backpack, Finn removed cans of pet food and portable dishes. After offering food and water to the escapees, he spread out a groundsheet and invited Chelsea to sit. She handed him a bottle of water and a snack. Tucking the kennel and dog close to them, they sat in a small circle.

"Hopefully we can find more," she said softly. "Or maybe some of the other searchers will."

Finn nodded. "They will be terrified. Poor things." Chelsea heard the love in his voice for these living creatures and it stirred her heart. Such a caring man. She shivered. He turned as she shifted position, his face mere inches from hers. His eyes sparkled in the night, sending a different kind of shiver down her spine. Her mouth parted of its own volition and then Finn's mouth was locked on hers, his sweet taste and gentle lip pressure doing crazy things to her heart and to be honest, her libido. She closed her eyes, willing the sensation to continue.

Suddenly, Finn drew away, and she opened her eyes, startled. He put a finger on his lips and touched his ear with the other hand. She strained to listen over the pounding of her heart. A whimper. Faint but there.

Finn indicated for her to stay still as he stood up. Taking the second kennel and a leash, he adjusted his headlamp and then moved silently toward the sound, pausing every few steps to listen. As he disappeared into the darkness, Chelsea put her lamp on low and hugged the trembling dog closer. "What's your name?" she wondered, moving her fingers around the collar, searching for tags. Peering at the one she found, she made out a word. "Leo?" she whispered. A small wag of his tail acknowledged his name. She pulled the small dog closer to her chest and let her chin rest on his head, enjoying the peace and warmth.

A howl sliced the night sky, followed by another, snapping her from her doze. Was that Finn? Or something else...something worse? The silence that ensued was worse than the noises themselves. She cuddled Leo closer and strained to hear. When her light caught Finn's shape appearing from the darkness, she expelled the breath she'd been holding. As he drew closer, she could see the kennel moving as he carried it.

"Thank goodness you're back!" Placing Leo gently by her feet, she hugged Finn as tightly as she could.

His face looked grim as he lowered the kennel to the ground then removed his backpack. "Coyotes found a few of the animals before I did. I have two dogs in the kennel. One's got a damaged leg. I did what I could for the others, but it was too late, I'm afraid." He swallowed hard. "These poor fellows are exhausted."

"Oh no." Chelsea moved to the kennel. Inside a German Shepherd cross and a black lab cross were smooshed together. The lab's front leg was wrapped, and she could see dark spots on his nose that were sure to be blood. She opened the door and neither dog moved. Finn handed her two small bowls of water that she placed by each animal's mouth. They lapped at it slowly but steadily. When they were done, she lifted the German Shepherd out of the kennel, and re-latched the door after ensuring the lab was comfortable. Clipping a leash to the German Shepherd's collar, she looked over at Finn for guidance.

"Let's head back." Finn drank deeply from his own water bottle. Laden as they were with the kennels, it took much longer on the return trip. Exhausted dogs on leashes didn't help either. The glow in the sky over the county shelter had lessened but firefighters were still on scene. She wept at the devastation – most of the shelter was gone.

As they loaded the animals into the clinic truck, one of the deputy chiefs approached them. "Thanks for your help," he said. "The other animals have been transported to your clinic." His soot-covered face looked tired, but his smile was genuine.

Finn shook the deputy chief's hand. "We'll take these ones over there now," he advised. "Any losses?"

The deputy chief grimaced. "Sadly, some of the cats. The fire started in the cattery. No known cause at this point. We'll take a few days to investigate. Gotta go. Thanks, again, Doc."

Chelsea smiled. "The new Doc, eh," she said to Finn. Finn grinned as he got into the driver's seat.

Finn was exhausted and glancing over at Chelsea, realized that she was as well. The animals in the back had quieted finally. He breathed a sigh of relief.

"Holy cow! Animals on the road! Hang on!"

Finn slammed the brakes as hard as he could and turned the wheel to the left. The action threw Chelsea forward and then back as her seat belt tightened. When the vehicle stopped, they were facing the ditch, parked sideways on the road.

"Are they okay?" Chelsea asked, her voice shocked.

Finn backed up the vehicle until the headlights illuminated the road ahead of them. A deer had been hit by a vehicle and killed, the body stark in the high beams. Huddled near it was a fawn, big eyes reflecting the light.

"Finn?" Chelsea breathed. "Do you think the baby is hurt?"

Finn shook his head. "I don't know. I'll go look." He started out of the vehicle and Chelsea opened her door as well.

"I'm coming with you." She hopped out before Finn could say no. Together, they crept towards the fawn, all the while talking softly. As they approached, the fawn sensed them and scampered onto unsteady legs. Finn couldn't see any damage to the small body or any visible blood. Loud barking shattered the stillness, causing the fawn to flee into the trees on the opposite side of the road.

Finn looked over at Chelsea. "Another shelter animal?"

Chelsea shrugged. "I'll go check," she said. Returning to the truck, she gathered her headlamp as well as a leash and her heavy gloves. Finn moved the truck to safety while she ventured into the woods. She could hear him chatting with Animal Control about the dead deer. So sad. Vehicles and roaming wildlife were never a good mix.

Casting her gaze as far as she could see, she made her way slowly through the trees. The barking had stopped but she could hear panting– the dog or dogs had to be close. Reaching into her pocket, she grabbed a handful of dog treats, intending to coax the lost wanderer. The next thing she knew, she was lying on the ground, breath knocked out of her. A huge dog slobbered over her, teeth grazing her palm where the treats had been. Grimacing from white-hot pain in her shoulder, she tried to rise and grab the dog's collar but suddenly, it bared its teeth and growled ominously. She wasn't going to win with this guy!

"Finn!" she yelled, with all the breath she could muster, her voice laced with pain. "Help!"

She could hear him running through the brush towards her. As he approached, the dog moved back, still growling, eyes glowing in the light of their headlamps. Finn followed the animal, chatting in a calm voice and moving slowly now.

"Be careful!" Chelsea managed. "He's a mean one!" She hated saying that about any animal, but this one was either hurt or starving or both. Any of those scenarios would make a dog furious. Trying to get up, she realized she'd smacked her shoulder against a gnarly stump. Excruciating pain radiated down her arm and side . She'd surely broken something.

Several seconds – or minutes later – Chelsea wasn't sure, Finn returned with a muzzle and leash on the dog. He gazed at her as he went by and realized instantly she was hurt. "Let me park this fellow in the truck and I'll come right back," he promised.

Chelsea closed her eyes. What a night. Warm tears ran down her face as she struggled again to sit up. Wasn't happening. She tried not to think about the pain in her shoulder and arm, concentrating instead on the sweet animals they'd rescued, even sending a prayer for the last mean one. She sent good wishes after the poor fawn, which made her cry more.

"Chels, I'm here," Finn said. He crouched beside her. "What hurts?" he asked, softly, his eyes moving across her body.

"My shoulder, my arm, " she whispered, her words broken by grunts of pain.

Finn paused for a moment. "I'm going to carry you to the truck. I'll wrap you in a blanket to stabilize your shoulder in case it's dislocated. Okay? Then I'll take you to the hospital."

"Okay," she agreed, then closed her eyes once more.

On the way home from the hospital, all Finn could think about was Chelsea. Her arm was broken just below the shoulder and her shoulder dislocated. She'd stay in the hospital the rest of the night. Craig had met him in the hospital parking lot to trade trucks and take the rescued animals to the temporary shelter at the clinic. Ashamed of his earlier annoyance at his new partner, Finn thanked him profusely and repeatedly.

Craig merely smiled and clapped him on the back, a knowing look on his face. "She's special to you," Craig said. "Anyone can see that. My pleasure to help out."

Finn's face flamed. Did everyone know how he felt about Chelsea? Why was he having such a hard time admitting it to himself?

When had things gotten so screwed up? Maybe when she told you she forgave you and you brushed it off? I was mad. Yeah, she said she forgave me but it was me who needed to forgive her for blaming me in the first place.

And have you?

Had he? The fear in his heart he'd felt when he'd realized she was hurt in the woods eclipsed every other feeling in his body. He loved this woman with all the parts of his being. He couldn't imagine a life without her. With a blinding jolt, Finn realized he had forgiven her. He'd truly forgiven her a long time ago.

Is it yourself you need to forgive, then? Do you blame yourself too?

Crikey! Finn slammed his hand on the steering wheel. He indeed blamed himself. He'd thought he'd put it behind him but deep down, he believed what Chelsea had believed – that if he or they had been there that night, they could have stopped Chance from driving, therefore saving his life.

Blast it all anyway. I didn't need her forgiveness – I needed my own.

Yup, you got it. You needed your own. Ding! Ding! Give the man a prize!

He headed to his place in town. When he walked into the almost bare apartment, he felt nothing. It wasn't home, it wasn't anything. Just like him without Chelsea.

He needed her in his life. He'd been a fool to pull away. He thought he was protecting himself, protecting her. All he was doing was hurting them both.

He had to fix this. And soon. But how?

Sinking onto the couch in the living room, his head in his hands, he contemplated his next steps. Yes, he desperately needed a shower and some food but those became minor compared to the mountain of a mess he'd made with Chelsea. And his plan. The plan that had backfired big time. Hiring Craig would become an issue if Craig didn't want to do any out-of-town calls - Finn had hired him to do the in-town work only. *Seemed like a good idea at the time.* He'd have to approach Craig and see if they could work out a different deal – maybe half and half, at least to start. Or offer to break their contract. Finn couldn't bear the thought of being away from Chelsea for that many hours each week. Even if it meant losing Craig for the clinic.

Of course, *if* Chelsea wouldn't believe that he really did love her, it didn't matter either way. He still owed it to Craig to be transparent and professional. It was the least he could do.

Through his own foolhardiness, Chelsea thought he didn't love her anymore. Would she ever forgive him for lying to her? He needed support. Maybe her family could help. Searching through his phone, he found Ryker's cell number. Hands shaking, he pressed the numbers.

"Hey there, Ryker, Finn here," he said. "I screwed up big time and I wonder if you could help me figure out how to make it right?"

Finn could hear Ryker pause, then a loud guffaw. "Let me take a wild stab at it...Chelsea?"

Finn nodded before remembering he was on the phone.

"Yes. Chelsea. I need help fast... "

For the next several minutes, he listened to Ryker's suggestions. When they finally hung up, Finn smiled to himself. He had a new plan. Now he needed to convince Chelsea that he was the man for her.

Easier said than done.

Chapter Eight

The next few days brought clear skies and sunshine. Chelsea had to spend a few weeks sleeping on her recliner so as not to disturb her broken arm. She hadn't seen Finn since he'd taken her to the hospital – she needed to thank him and so much more. Bored after a week in the apartment, sleeping and healing, she walked over to the clinic. Finn's company truck was missing but she assumed he'd gone out on a call. She was too busy introducing Craig to local pet owners for the next while as they showed up for their appointments to think about Finn. She did learn that Finn and Craig had done emergency surgeries on the injured animals she and Finn had rescued, as well as the ones rescued by other members of the community. Their recovery area was full but it looked like all of them would survive.

The staff from the county shelter had taken care of the animals relocated from the fire. She was grateful for their help and happy that the new shelter was complete enough to accommodate all of the animals. While she was in her office, she worked out a schedule for 24/7 staffing for the shelter, made easier by the fact that most of the current shelter workers were willing to continue employment with Finn and Chelsea.

After a few hours, she asked for a ride to the McCoy ranch. She needed to go somewhere to clear her head, and home was always a good place to start. Sammy dropped her off out front and Chelsea breathed deeply of the air on the ranch. She headed into the kitchen, not passing anyone on the way. She glanced out the window, seeing Mac's wheelchair and a few of the ranch workers – and was that Finn? Why on earth would he be here? Unless there was a problem with one of the ranch horses? She stepped carefully into a pair of rubber boots from the back door cubbies before heading out. As she rounded the corner of the house, she saw Mac rolling her way, with Ryker at his side. No one else. She must be imagining things, she thought. Yikes.

"Hey broken-arm girl," yelled Mac. "What brings you to the ranch?"

Ignoring him, Chelsea stepped into a warm hug from Ryker, melting into his familiar embrace. Brothers may not always be good for much, but the hugs were a godsend.

"You doing okay?" Ryker asked, holding her face in his hands to examine it. "You look tired. How's the arm?"

Chelsea swallowed the tears that crept into her throat and shook her head. "No, I'm not okay," she admitted, swiping at the few tears that escaped her eyes. "My arm hurts and I..."

'Wanna sit and talk about it?" Mac offered. Ryker nodded. "We have time now if you like."

Chelsea leaned over carefully, enveloping Mac in a big one-armed hug. "I could really use some brotherly advice, thanks."

A while later, sitting in the front living room, after spilling her guts and ending with "So that's that," she felt better.

Her brothers looked at each other and then Ryker said, "And you are good with that?"

"No, but what else can I do? I really do love him. I've spent so many years blaming him for Chance's death. And now it's too late. He fell out of love with me." Tears streamed down her face again.

Ryker rose to get her a new box of tissues. "Hmm," he said. "That's unfortunate. What are your plans then?"

Chelsea stared at him. "Plans? I have no plans. I'm locked into a business agreement with a man who barely tolerates me and who I still love. Not really a win-win from where I'm sitting."

Mac nodded. "Yeah, I can see that. Would talking to him about it again work, do you think?"

Chelsea shook her head. "I wish it would but I seriously doubt it."

Mac persisted. "But if it could work, what would you say to him?"

Chelsea groaned. "I'd ask him to forgive me for blaming him in the first place, then ask if there was anything I could do to earn his love again."

Mac nodded. "Good start."

"But Mac, I doubt if he will even talk to me."

Ryker jumped in. "Chels, you never know what goes through a man's mind. All I can tell you is that love, once given, seldom disappears. Pride, hurt, fear – those things come into play to mask that love but the love is still there, deep down."

Chelsea stared at him. "That sounds like you know exactly what I'm going through. Something happening that I don't know about, Ryk?"

Ryker smiled. "We all have our secrets. All I meant was that sometimes love hides behind other emotions."

"Why don't you give him some space before you talk to him again? He probably needs time to process what's happening and realize the truth himself," Mac advised.

"Good plan. Thanks, guys. Tears aside, it feels good to share that with you. I appreciate your ears. And your lack of judgment." She glared pointedly at Mac, her biggest critic when they were younger. He just laughed.

"Time to go. Can you drive me home, Ryk?" As she rose, she caught movement outside the big south window. "Who was that?"

Ryker glanced outside. "I don't see anyone," he remarked. "Are you sure that you're all right?"

Chelsea slapped his arm with her good hand. "Yes, I think I am." He grinned and patted her head.

The next morning, as she walked to the clinic, she noticed a sign on the path to the temporary shelter structure. 'Path closed for maintenance.'

Craig was not in, so she and Gloria handled the morning clients. After lunch, Craig was handling two surgeries then a last-minute rabbit incident that resulted in them working late. It was dark by the time she locked the clinic doors.

Walking past the path to the rescue, she noticed the sign she'd seen earlier was down. She could see twinkling lights lining the pathway. Making sure her Maglite was in her pocket in case she needed more light, she walked along the path. A tarp had been thrown over the geometric dome, but she could see faint light from within. The doors to the temporary structure were locked, as were the ones to the permanent shelter.

That's so odd, what is going on?

"Good evening."

She squealed. Jeepers creepers! She almost jumped out of her skin.

"Finn?" she whispered to the dark shape in the shadows.

"Yes, it's me. Come on in, I want to show you something." He disappeared further into the darkness.

Chelsea crept forward, reaching with her good arm to move the tarp so she could go inside. She barely touched the tarp when it slid right out of her hand and completely off the dome. Her breath caught in her throat as she gazed inside. Fairy lights lit every part of the dome, twinkling in a myriad of colors. A portable fireplace was set up on one side, with a thick furry rug on the hearth and thick fluffy blankets. A glass table set for two – champagne with elegant crystal flutes, roses everywhere, a tray of charcuterie, and strawberries dipped in chocolate.

And Finn. Her heart trembled.

Finn wore pressed black jeans with a long-sleeved black sweater molded to his torso. He stepped forward and took her hand, leading her to a comfortable-looking chair beside the glass table.

"Welcome," his voice was just above a whisper.

"What is this?" Chelsea asked, confused.

"This, Chelsea, my love, is an apology, an affirmation, and a proposal rolled into one."

What? Was he joking with her? She lifted her eyes to his and saw nothing but shining love. For her.

Her heart beat wildly and her breath caught in her throat.

"I thought you didn't love me anymore. Remember?"

Finn shrugged as he leaned over to fill her champagne flute.

"Hmm. About that..."

Chelsea held her breath and waited. One second turned into two, turned into ten, turned into an eternity.

Finn knelt on the ground beside her, close enough to touch. Her hand inched toward him and she pressed it into her thigh to keep it still. She didn't dare interrupt this moment.

"Chelsea, I love you. I loved you yesterday. I love you today and I will love you all the tomorrows that we are gifted. I have never stopped loving you."

Chelsea let out a ragged breath.

"Why did you say you didn't love me anymore then?" A tear slipped down her cheek.

Finn gently touched the tear with his fingers.

"I lied," he said simply. "I was hurting and frustrated, and I didn't know what to do. I thought it would be better to stay away. I thought that was what you wanted. So I lied."

Chelsea gazed into his eyes and something shifted deep inside as if their souls connected.

"And how did that work out for you?" she teased.

Finn chuckled and kissed her. "Not well," he admitted. And kissed her again.

He took her hands in his.

"Chelsea, darling Chelsea. I love you with all my heart. Will you please forgive me and marry me before I do something even more stupid?"

He opened his hand, a sparkling engagement ring on his palm. The one she'd thrown back at him after Chance died. The one she'd said she didn't want.

She paused, taking in every inch of his beautiful kind loving face. Her Finn.

"Yes, yes, I will."

He gazed at her swollen left hand for a moment, then without missing a beat, he reached for her right hand. "This one will do," he said, as he slid the ring onto the ring finger.

She stood, leaning into his embrace, soaking up his essence, his Finn-ness, his strength, his warmth, his love.

The fairy lights seemed to pause for a moment then sparkle more brightly, as if the universe, or maybe her departed twin, wholeheartedly approved.

Chelsea smiled at Finn with happy tears in her eyes.

"Chance sends his blessing," she whispered. "I love you, Finn."

"Thanks, Chance," Finn said seriously. They raised their flutes to the sky and gave a silent toast to the man they'd lost and the love they'd finally found again together, forever.

Chelsea paused. "Oh," she said, covering her mouth with one hand. "I forgot..."

Finn stepped back, a look of angst on his face. "Oh, please don't change your mind..."

"Oh no, I won't do that," she laughed. "But I do have to tell you about Leo."

Finn groaned. "Another man?"

Chelsea grinned. "Kind of," she concurred. "But I think you'll like this one. He's going to be part of our family."

She pressed her lips against his once again.

The End

About Lynn Gale

Lynn Gale has dreamed about writing romance ever since she read *If This Is Love* by Anne Weale in 1972. Years went by and she fell in love with romance all over again watching movies like ***Romancing the Stone***, ***American Dreamer***, and ***Pride and Prejudice.***

Her first sweet romance novella *A Heart Creek Christmas* was published in 2023 as part of ***A Cowboy This Christmas: A Sweet Romance Anthology*** through the Calgary Association of Romance Writers of America (CaRWA) under the pen name Joanie Wilde. This novella will be released as a stand alone title in February 2025.

A Heart Creek Second Chance can be read as a stand alone title and also as part of the ongoing series ***Return to Heart Creek***.

Romances by Lynn Gale

Return to Heart Creek Series

A Heart Creek Christmas (Feb 2025)*

*currently available in *A Cowboy for Christmas: A Sweet Romance Anthology*Written as Joanie Wilde

After a disastrous ride leaves former rodeo champion Mac McCoy unable to compete, he reluctantly agrees to move back home to Heart Creek. Bitter and broken, he is shocked to discover feelings for equine osteopath Carrie Saunders. As he struggles to find acceptance of a new way of life that does not include rodeos, he fights his growing attraction to Carrie believing that she needs a whole man, not a broken-down cowboy. Former massage therapist Carrie Saunders is looking forward to a new adventure in her chosen field of equine osteopathy. Avidly opposed to rodeos, she finds purpose in treating and healing retired rodeo horses. Her dream job opportunity brings her to a ranch in Alberta for a six-month contract. Somehow former rodeo champion Mac McCoy sneaks into her heart leaving her wondering how to stay true to her beliefs while falling in love with the cowboy. Is Mac her soulmate, or the man who will destroy her heart?

A Heart Creek Second Chance (April 2024)

Finn Buchanan returns to Heart Creek to realize his dream: taking over the local veterinarian practice even though he knows it means facing his former fiancée, Chelsea McCoy. When her brother died six years ago, Chelsea blamed him and called off their engagement. They haven't spoken since. He is shocked to discover he still loves her and when their paths cross to devise a solution for a local shelter's issues, he struggles to maintain his distance while working together for a community solution. Animal Health Technician – and Heart Creek McCoy – Chelsea McCoy stumbles onto a solution for a local shelter's problem. It does mean working with her former fiancé Finn Buchanan. Chelsea blames him for the death of her brother and has been unable to move past the tragedy that occurred. Can she get past her anger and resentment to work with Finn to create a solution for the shelter's problems? He's already broken her heart once – will he do it again, or can they work in harmony for the good of the community and let the past be in the past.

A Heart Creek Reunion (Nov 2024)

Reunited with her family in Heart Creek, recently widowed mom of twin boys, Avery McCoy Dushane, seeks solace after the sudden death of her husband Josh. Avery is surprised and terrified to find herself attracted to new veterinarian Craig Willmott, a committed bachelor. Craig feels the same way about her but their road to romance is as rocky as the last year of Avery's marriage, filled with Craig's reluctance to commit, and Avery's guilt about falling in love so soon after her husband's death.

A Heart Creek Wedding (Feb 2025)

Ryker McCoy feels that love has passed him by until he meets firefighter/wedding planner Lynsey Adams. Ryker always thought of himself as an equal opportunity guy but from the onset, Lynsey's protective services career choice brings out the worst in him. For her part, Lynsey finds him rude and overbearing, not to mention chauvinistic. From their first meeting at the wedding rehearsal for Mac and Carrie's wedding to a fire incident at the McCoy Ranch, sparks fly and tensions swirl. Can they both get past their first impressions and realize their love for one another, or will the passion die a slow death before it even burns bright?

Lynn's Social Links

Email: lynngalewriter@gmail.com
Website: https://www.lynngalewriter.com
Facebook: http://www.facebook.com/lynngalewriter
Instagram: http://www.instagram.com/lynngalewriter
Bookbub: https://www.bookbub.com/profile/lynn-gale

Acknowledgements

This book would not have been possible without the assistance and support of many people in my life.

My mentor romance author Katie O'Connor, who has been instrumental in guiding me through the process of learning to write. She is my first reader and I am truly grateful for her direction and support, and for introducing me to my editor and my writing software Atticus.

My editor Terri St. Clair, for her thoughtful comments and excellent editing.

My cover designer Laura Heritage of P.S. Cover Design & Author Services for the gorgeous covers for the Return to Heart Creek series.

My family for their love and support. I love you all so much!

My sister Anne – remember when we wanted to be authors? It's happening!

My super fan and dear friend Anne Marie – yes, there is a fine line between fan and stalker!

My amazing island bestie Pat – miss you always.

My readers – without you, these are just words on a page. Thank you for your support and for hanging in there with me while I develop my craft.

xxoo Lynn